THE
STAR

Also by David Skibbins

EIGHT OF SWORDS
HIGH PRIESTESS

THE STAR

DAVID SKIBBINS

THOMAS DUNNE BOOKS
ST. MARTIN'S MINOTAUR
NEW YORK

Skibbins

This is a work of fiction. All of the characters, organizations, and events portrayed in this novel are either products of the author's imagination or are used fictitiously.

THOMAS DUNNE BOOKS
An imprint of St. Martin's Press.

www.thomasdunnebooks.com
www.stmartins.com

Library of Congress Cataloging-in-Publication Data Available upon Request

ISBN-13: 978-0-312-36193-8
ISBN-10: 0-312-36193-9

First Edition: February 2007

10 9 8 7 6 5 4 3 2 1

I dedicated my first two books to organizations and women that many people know. The Star is dedicated to a woman very few people know. You can't even find **Dorothea Romankiw** *by searching in Google. And yet, for dozens of us, she altered our lives completely. She died in her eighties in July of 2006.*

In 1964 she began a treatment center for schizophrenic adolescents based on the work of Carl Jung called St. George Homes. It was located in Victorian houses scattered around north Berkeley. She was brilliant, impossible, unpredictable, compassionate, and rarely satisfied. But she woke up the staff, and some of the kids, to a magical, mystical world of myth and beauty that permeates what we call ordinary reality. Jungians study the collective unconscious. At St. George's we lived it. In tepees on the desert floor, in sweat lodges under redwoods, in candlelight beside a frozen lake, or dressed in robes and ornate masks in the hills of Berkeley, one hundred and fifty staff and forty-five schizophrenic teenagers encountered the healing power of the collective unconscious. One young patient said it best: "In other institutions people watched me go down into the crazy places. You went down there with me, by my side. Then we came out together."

It is because of her that Warren knows these dark corners of the psyche. He, and I, bow low in honor of your memory, Dorothea.

ACKNOWLEDGMENTS

Well, if it takes a village to raise a child, it takes a small municipality to foster a novel. I am in debt to the usual crew, my personal readers and editors: Laura Kennedy and P. J. Coldren, and the stellar crew at St. Martin's—Ruth Cavin, Toni Plummer, and the other fantastic editorial, production, marketing, and promotional staff who got this puppy from inception to your hands. Warren and I raise a glass to my career-building agent, Jennifer Jackson. Kudos also to Joel and Jeremy Crockett at Four-Eyed Frog Books, and to all other dedicated independent booksellers who do such a great job finding each of us exactly the right book to read. And, of course, to you, dear reader. I am your humble servant, good for a joke or two, a poem, a few songs, and a good tale for your entertainment. Thank you for your patronage.

My daughter, mother, and father continue to be my most fanatical supporters. And finally, to my wife, Marla, I have this to say:

At the end of every manuscript, I type "The End,"
and thank God that we have many more chapters together.

SUNDAY, DECEMBER 18

And in despair I bowed my head
"There is no peace on earth," I said,
"For hate is strong and mocks the song
Of peace on earth, good will to men."

Then pealed the bells more loud and deep:
"God is not dead, nor doth He sleep;
The wrong shall fail, the right prevail
With peace on earth, good will to men."

—"I Heard the Bells on Christmas Day,"
Henry W. Longfellow (1864)

CHAPTER ONE

Mr. Ritter, I mean Warren, ah . . . Dad, I need your help."

One, she'd never called me "Dad" before. Two, she looked like hell. Three, she'd never asked for help. I knew I was in big trouble.

"Fran, hi! Wow, you don't look so good. What's wrong?"

Tears welled up in her eyes. She gulped, but couldn't talk.

"Hey, I'm guessing this isn't a conversation for the middle of Telegraph Avenue, is it?"

"Well no, not really."

"Let me close up, and we'll go get some coffee."

To close up my shop all I had to do was stuff my tarot cards into a bag and fold up my table. As I gathered my deck up, one card fell on the sidewalk. A little nervously I bent over to pick it up. Please, no bad omens. Whew. It was the image of a nude woman pouring water into a pool, with large radiant stars shining overhead: the Star card. I had no idea what it meant to me. At least it wasn't the Death card.

I took down my Day-Glo sign that read, *Love? Success? Money? Your Answer Is in the Cards! Discover the Truth. Tarot Cards Readings Here.* I bungee-corded it to the card table and tucked them both under one arm. Then I grabbed the two extra-heavy-duty folding chairs. I trooped into Cody's Books, with Fran right behind me. It was almost as though she wanted to make sure I didn't slip away from her. I tucked my portable office into my reserved corner of the staff room. Within two minutes I was back on the avenue, strolling with my daughter toward the Mediterraneum Caffé.

Christmas was just a week off. I was walking away from one of the most lucrative days of the year. Berkeley was jammed. Cal freshman looked for gross and bizarre gifts they could bring home to shock their parents. An ex-hippie therapist pawed through the racks, on the quest for some tie-dye bunting for her grandchildren. A guy who looked like an Old Testament prophet, and smelled like he had spent way too long in the desert, sat behind a sign that read: *Give me money, I'm crazy!* And a stream of translucent bubbles floated across our path, streaming behind the Bubble Lady as she wandered through the crowds and hawked her latest self-published book of poetry. Holiday season on the open ward, and I was missing it.

But I had to deal with Fran. After all, she'd called me "Dad." Fatherhood was a very new gig for me. I'd spent most of my adult life on the run, underground from law enforcement and out of sight of my one-time radical compatriots. Folks thought I'd blown myself up in 1970, and I'd done everything I could do since then to foster that belief.

I didn't even know I had a daughter until this year. And a grandkid, too. Not that I'd ever met him. Fran kept me distant from her personal life. She trusted me about as much as I trusted

4

the president. This was only the third time we'd ever met face to face. She was just as new to daughterhood, and was in no hurry to embrace her good old dad. Until today.

The balcony in the café was empty except for one white kid with Rastafarian dreadlocks, lost in his iPod, as he nursed his tiny cup of espresso. The pierced punks and their junkyard dogs lounged on the sidewalk in front of the café. They provided local color and successfully frightened off everyone but the regulars. Fran and I carried our double lattes to an unsteady and undersized table near the railing. We sat there in silence for a couple of sips.

"Orrin—you remember—he's my husband? He just took Justin away from me."

I'd never met Orrin either. But I was already predisposed to disapprove of him. He was a cop. "That's bull. Nobody can do that, even if he is a cop. Your boy's—what—six months old, right? Where's Justin now?"

Fran took a gulp of hot coffee big enough to scald her mouth. It seemed to have no effect.

"He's five months and six days old. He's with Orrin's folks in Watsonville. Orrin is living there too, I think." Then she was silent. She stared out vacantly at the café below. Silence for a while. I didn't know what to say.

When she spoke next she seemed like she was talking in a dream. "The house was so quiet after they left. I couldn't stand it. I took a walk out to Steamers Point. I sat and watched two crows work over a robin's nest. The first crow harassed the mom so bad that she flew up to chase it off. As soon as she was away from the nest, crow number two zoomed in. He chipped a hole in an egg and savored the baby inside like an appetizer. Then he took another egg in his black claws and dropped it on the hard earth below. His buddy soared down and feasted on that baby. The mother bird came back to the nest, cleaned out the broken eggshells, and settled back down to brood on whatever was left."

This conversation was not going in a positive, cocreative direction. I had to pull her attention out of her private dismal swamp. "Fran, over here. Enough with the crows, already. Look at me! There you go! Now how can that happen? A father can't take a baby away from his mother. You can fight this!"

She looked at me with holocaust eyes. "I've been pretty angry and confused lately. He's got some pictures of bruises on Justin. I left a few bruises on Orrin, too. He's got a witness who saw me kind of lose track of Justin one day at Macy's. I just didn't pay very good attention that day. You know how that goes."

I did know how that goes. I'd passed down my genetic curse to her: bipolar disorder. I had first-hand experience with how it could make life very disorderly. I nodded. Those pesky delusions.

"Orrin could have turned me in to Child Protective Services and they'd take Justin away. But he made a deal with me. If I let him take Justin, and didn't make a fuss, then he'd keep Social Services out of it. What could I do? Hell, he's a cop. He could arrest me himself for abuse and neglect."

This was a mess, no question about it. But why was it dumped in my lap?

"Fran, I want to help. I will help. But I've got a couple of questions. Where is your mother?"

"Grams fell and broke her hip. Mom's doing a twenty-four/seven with her. She suggested that I come to you."

Thanks a lot! I thought to myself. But I smiled at Fran. "OK, how about Aunt Tara?" For decades my sister thought I'd been killed in that explosion. This year she accidentally unearthed me

6

and discovered that I had been rambling around incognito all that time. She was still angry at me. But she was very close to Fran.

"Don't talk to me about your sister. She's a judgmental bitch, and I'm not about to talk to her!"

OK, then. That explained it. I was all that was left. Not an atypical situation for us manic-depressives. We have a tendency to periodically dynamite our support system. But this situation was too big for little old fugitive me! I wanted some support here.

"I'm right here for you, Fran. But I think we might need some help. Is there someone in Santa Cruz who might help us straighten all this out?"

"My pastor, Larry Dalton, maybe. He's a sweetie. But he's my husband's pastor, too. Or at least he was. Orrin stopped going to church lately. Anyway Larry's known Orrin since they were kids. So I don't know whose side he is on. His wife is great, too. Maybe they can help. I don't know."

"Look, Fran, I'll do what I can. I can come down to Santa Cruz right now, if that's what you need. But I also know that you need to get on some meds. What you're going through won't shift until you get your moods stabilized. Believe me, I've been there!"

She stood up and slammed her empty latte glass on the table. The fog in her eyes turned to glistening metal. I put up my hands in case she decided to pick the glass back up and chuck it at me. Instead she yelled, "I'm not crazy! You're just like all the rest of them! There's nothing wrong with me. You probably want to lock me up just like everybody else. Well, fuck you! I don't need your fucking help anyway. I know how to handle this myself! Fucking bastard!" She stalked off, ignoring my pleas to come back and sit down and talk things out.

A couple of people in the café looked up briefly. Then they

7

went back to their newspapers. After Reagan shut down the state mental hospital system, screaming tantrums became daily occurrences on Telegraph. That's why everyone who doesn't live here thinks it's cute to call this place Bezerkley.

I watched Fran slam the front door, kick aside a scrounger on the sidewalk, and stride off. There goes my baby. Boy, I sure handled that interaction masterfully. Dad of the Year Award Ceremony, here I come.

CHAPTER TWO

I felt like crap after mangling my coffee klatch with Fran. I hate to be called crazy and I just did that to her. What an idiot!

I didn't want to go back to work. The holiday spirit had given up the ghost. I walked out of the café and looked up and down the avenue. It looked like the Grunge gang stole Christmas. The homeless, the psychotic, the drug dealers and all their ravenous clients wandered among the throng of middle-class Santa's elves. There was a frantic grasping in the air. Hungry ghosts were clamoring for prettier baubles, and better highs.

I walked through it like an alien. My heart didn't flutter at the thought of buying those glittering earrings or that leather pouch. I didn't imagine the squeals of delight as some poor soul ripped open the wrapping paper and pulled out rainbow-colored socks with cannabis leaves embroidered on them. Scrooge had nothing on me this afternoon.

I didn't know what to make of Christmas anymore. Christmas was for families. I'd deserted my family after a townhouse blew up in Greenwich Village. During the decades that I was on the run my father died and my mother sank into Alzheimer's.

For thirty years I set up alternative identities and moved on whenever I thought the FBI might get a clue to where I was, or whenever relationships got too messy or too intense. I'd expected to go through life that way: unattached. Until this year hit.

Now I had a girlfriend, a teenager who wished I was her dad, a sister who often wished I was dead, a daughter, and a grandson. Kind of like attachment disorder in reverse, I had too much of a good thing.

I headed into the university. The grounds were all but deserted during winter break, which suited me just fine. I saw a couple of indiscriminately gendered graduate students, in a rush to the library to get one last reference for their Review of the Literature sections of their pointless dissertations. Holidays for those poor Cratchetts were just times of restricted library hours.

Once past the library I was on my own. My only company was a motley crew of critters: Two crows just up from an egg feast in Santa Cruz did barrel loops, a blue jay worried a candy wrapper, and one scroungy brown dog wandered, lonely for the usual troop of students who could be relied upon to drop food. I called him over, maybe a little lonely myself. Once he saw I had no lunch, he stopped. Then he headed away, toward Telegraph Avenue and better pickings.

I decided I needed a geographic antidepressant. I dropped in to Black Oak Books to browse. The best way to do a bookstore is to let the force be with you. I just wandered. I let this title or that dust jacket pull me in one direction or another. I only own seven books at any one time, but these days I was down to six, which meant there was a vacancy to be filled.

I debated between *The Shame of the Nation: The Restoration of*

Apartheid Schooling in America by Jonathan Kozol and *All Mortal Flesh*, a mystery by Julia Spencer-Fleming. I was sitting on one of the chairs at the end of a set of shelves, leafing through the Spencer-Fleming book, when a man cleared his throat in a "Please look up at me" way.

He was a small, trim old guy, a good head of gray hair still, and missing the stooped shoulders that so many older men have. He was in a royal blue oxford shirt with French cuffs, dark gray wool slacks, and sensible, but well-polished, black leather shoes. And right now he looked very pale.

"Yes?"

"I'm sorry. I feel very awkward right now. But I couldn't stop looking at you." He spoke in a precise American accent, reminiscent of Princeton professors. "You bear an uncanny resemblance to a very dear friend of mine. Ex-friend, actually, he's long dead. It's like seeing his ghost. I hate to bother you, but are you any relation to Walter Green?"

Here's a hint: Go ahead when you're young and spend a couple of grand to get plastic surgery on your face; restructure your nose, raise those cheekbones, and color your hair. Just don't expect it to last for thirty years. After a while age and gravity tend to erase all those alterations. Then you're back to an old version of your original face. This was the second time this year someone tagged me as my pre-hegira self.

Sure, Walter Green was my father. Not that I was ready to tell this guy anything. He was too old to be FBI, but he was still a stranger.

"Why do you ask?"

"You're Richard, aren't you? He always said you didn't die in that explosion. Oh my."

I didn't like the way this little chat was going. "Look buddy, this is a case of mistaken identity. My name ain't Richard. I don't know any Wally Green, and he sure ain't my father. Sorry."

The clean old man looked me over carefully. Then he took a card out of his wallet and handed it to me. "I understand, Richard. But there are things I can tell you about your father that you never knew. So, when you are ready, give me a call."

I took his card, denying it all the way. "Ah, thanks, buddy, but you're way off base here. I don't know you or your Mr. Green at all."

He smiled. Then he said, "And tonight, when you go to bed, turn over that steel Omega Chronograph watch you're wearing. You will see etched on the back the initials E.L. and W.G."

He turned and walked away. I looked down at his card. It read ERIC LANDON, PORT COSTA and had a phone number. I needed a drink.

CHAPTER THREE

Who the hell is Eric Landon?"

"That's what I asked you."

It was another one of those fun and productive calls between me and my sister, Tara. When she discovered me on the streets of Berkeley she almost had a cow. All those decades she had to take care of my Alzheimer's mother alone. She had to emotionally support my pregnant girlfriend and then her daughter. She had to manage the grief of my death and later my father's death. Meanwhile, her brother was tootling all over the United States on his motorcycle playing the Fugitive. Our reunion has been a rocky one.

One small sign of the break-up of the Arctic ice cap happened last month, when she gave me a watch from Dad's belongings. She wanted me to have something from him, little realizing that it was a Judas watch that would betray me.

Tara said, "I never heard of this guy. Dad never mentioned him. Are you sure you're not being conned, or that maybe you misheard him?"

This was my sister's delicate way of indicating that perhaps I had hallucinated the whole event, or I'd woven a benign interaction into some delusional pattern. She didn't understand bipolar disorders, and happily confused them with schizophrenia. Not that I haven't had a few delusional moments. Just ask my therapist, Rose. But for the past few years I had done a darn good job at managing my medication to exorcise those demons. I was in a rock steady mental state these days, and was darn sure that Eric Landon wasn't a product of my psychopathology.

"No, Tara. It's all real. Too damn real. Those initials are etched into this watch. That's irrefutable fact. There's only one way this guy could know that. He did it. Maybe he's a jeweler. What was the name of Dad's bimbo second wife?"

"No luck there. Her name was Julia Hightower. So just call up this guy if you want to find out what's going on."

"OK, Sis. I'll check it out."

"Oh and Richard," she refused to use my assumed name, "I don't really care that much about Dad and his little adventures. Don't feel like you need to tell me every sordid detail. In fact, maybe you should just forget the whole thing. That would be my recommendation."

Click.

My sister often reminds me of the White Witch from *The Lion, the Witch, and the Wardrobe*. She loved the winter of our discontent, and wasn't going to warm things up anytime soon. I wasn't about to drop this. It was time to bell the cat.

I dialed the number on the card, hoping to get an answering machine. Damn cell phones; my bookstore gentleman immediately picked up. "Eric Landon here."

14

"Hello, Eric. This is the guy you met at the bookstore tonight."
I was a little embarrassed at my failed attempt at deception.

"Oh, hello, Richard."

Damn, I hated that name cropping up all the time. I'd spent thirty years running from it, but it just kept hanging on my heels.

"So, here's the deal, Eric; I may want to talk with you. But if I ever hear you use that Richard name again, I'm walking in the other direction, and you'll never see me again. *Capisce?*"

"That's no problem. What would you prefer that I call you?"

I didn't want him connecting to my identity as Warren Ritter. He just knew too damn much already. "Call me Ishmael."

He laughed. "All right, Ishmael. I should like to talk with you about your—um—about Walter Green."

"Good recovery there, Eric. When?"

"I could meet you in two hours at the Roma Café on Ashby."

Wow, that was way fast. I took a deep breath and said, "Sure."

CHAPTER FOUR

Roma Café was an archetypal Berkeley coffee shop. The coffee came in bathtub-sized cups, the salads were organic right down to the balsamic vinegar, and someone there would be reading the *Times* (either New York or London, but never Los Angeles). It was a rare night that you didn't hear several languages contributing to the cacophony. I found Eric in the back room, a slightly quieter place to hide. There were two huge cups before him.

"I presupposed. You do like lattes, correct, Ishmael?"

"Another genetic trait?"

"I'm afraid so. He drank them constantly. I have to switch to decaf after five, but your father could drink espresso at midnight and sleep like a dog in the summer heat."

I drank. He drank. Neither one of us wanted to start. It was kind of eerie. He kept looking at me with these wide-open eyes. I imagined he wasn't seeing me at all, only a memory.

Finally I said, "How did you know my father?"

A very large sigh from such a small man. "Ishmael, I am afraid there is much you do not know about your father."

This man began to annoy me. "Well, I know that he beat me, and that he was a vicious bastard to my mother sometimes, and that my sister adored him anyway. I know that he deserted us completely, except to pay generous child support. I think I know him pretty well." I didn't mention how much I missed him, or how hard it had hit me to find out he had died.

"And did you know that he was gay?"

I was speechless. Time passed, I guess. Then I said, "No, sorry buddy. My sister and I are living proof that he liked women. Hell, he left my mother for some bimbo, or a number of bimbos. You're dead wrong." I started to get up to leave.

"Stop. Please give me a minute. I'm sorry. I misspoke. Your father was bisexual. He enjoyed having sex with a wide variety of people, men and women. I'm sorry to dump it on you like that. I know it must come as a big shock. I just don't really know how else to say it. Allow me to introduce myself. I am Eric Landon. I was your father's lover in the years before his death."

I was still standing. "No, no, no! He was married to someone named Julia. Let's get real here. I don't know what your game is, but it sure isn't working."

Eric looked sorry for me. He said gently, "Please sit."

I did, reluctantly. Then he said, "Yes, he did marry Julia Hightower. He was very flattered that a woman as young and intelligent as she was would fall for a guy in his late sixties. She told him she was in her thirties, so he wouldn't feel like he was robbing the cradle. But she was lying. My bet was she was closer to twenty than thirty. She was just a kid, but a good-looking racehorse, that's for sure.

"However, monogamy was not a strong suit for Walter. And he did cherish our relationship. So I became his 'mistress,' so to speak.

"Your father spoke often about you. He was very confused about why you seemed to abandon the values he thought he had instilled in you, and instead chose to join those hooligans."

I was getting really pissed. I didn't know if it was at Eric or my father. "Yes, great American values, like hitting your kids, treating your wife with contempt, running off with some fairy from the Castro. Do you blame me?"

"Actually I live in Port Costa, but point well taken. I'm sure he had plenty of fairies in the Castro before he found me. We were both remarkably lucky not to be HIV positive. I take it from your pale complexion that this comes as a shock. You obviously don't share your father's gender preferences."

I thought about his question.

On the "Heck no, I'm an all-American male!" side, I never fantasized about gay sex, and only dreamed about it a couple of times. When I was in the Weather Underground we decided that monogamy was a product of the paternalistic, capitalist oligarchy. We needed to smash that shibboleth, too. Every heterosexual pairing and many group ones were attempted. Only going steady was outlawed. No two people could pair off for any length of time without becoming subject to a grilling at our weekly Weatherfries pressure group.

Since the chicks were on the far left of the radical feminists of the sixties, most woman-woman pairings were consummated. But the guys stayed traditionally homophobic. We played with bombs, not with each other.

But then there was the fact that I kind of liked my job at Nordstrom, even though I bitched about it. In fact, I became the unofficial shopper for many cross-dressers at our store. It's hard, if you cross-dress, to go into either gender's dressing room to try on clothes. I got a reputation for being able to eyeball a guy and pick out his size in the women's section. I even put aside some of the larger dresses and blouses, the ones I thought would be perfect for "my gals." I decked those guys out pretty stylishly, if I do say so myself. Was it a genetic gift?

So I didn't really know what to tell Eric. "Mostly I'm a confirmed heterosexual. What can you tell me about my dad?"

"He was certainly *not* a confirmed heterosexual. He loved way too many guys. If you are Rich . . . I mean obviously you are . . . anyway, I have something for you."

What did I want from this guy? I felt ripped off by my father in so many ways, and this was one of the more twisted ones. He was still messing with me from his grave. It was time to get out of there.

He reached inside a leather portfolio that he had placed by the side of his chair. "I found this among his belongings. It was addressed to you. I assume he was going to give it to you if he ever met you. I haven't read it, but I've always been curious about what it said."

I took the envelope. "Look, Eric, I really don't know what to say. The man I knew as my father was a very different man from the person you slept with. And I am not in the mood for reminiscing. So, thank you for giving me this, and for the coffee. I'd best be going."

He was obviously disappointed. I guess I was as rude as my father. "Oh well, if you'd ever like to talk some more, I would be very happy to. It was very nice to see you. You look a lot like him. Not the nose, but the chin and your eyebrows. It's a bit uncanny—you're the age he was when I met him."

God, I was getting claustrophobic! "Well, it's quite remarkable meeting you also. I'll probably call sometime next year. If only to assuage your curiosity about the letter." There. Now I'd done my good deed. I'd made nice-nice with the old goat. I could go. And find a fine and private place to rip open that envelope and find out what was inside. Rose always told me I had the impulse control of a four-year-old. And, as usual, she was right.

As I got up to discreetly storm out Eric dropped his last bombshell. "There's one more thing you should know. That heart attack of your father's: There's something very suspicious about it. He never told me about any problem with his heart. It came out of the blue. I think that bears looking into."

"I'm not a private eye. Go talk to the police."

"Oh, I did. They were not interested in the ranting of an old fag."

Right now, I wasn't either. "Sorry, Eric. I have to leave now."

CHAPTER FIVE

y bed would have done nicely as a place to read the scarlet letter, or in this case, the lavender letter. But my car was closer. It would have to do. I parked under a streetlight and tore the envelope open.

Dear Richard:

If you're reading this, I was right all along. I'm writing this on March 6th, 1990, exactly twenty years since you were supposedly destroyed in an explosion. I will never forget that week from hell. I flew back east to support your mother and sister, and to deal with the press and the police. What a god-awful mess. But all the time I wondered if you'd faked your death. All they ever found were pieces of your wallet and your jacket. No fingers or body parts that looked remotely like yours. I know, because they dragged me in to look at some of the pieces they'd recovered.

Finally, I caught on. A father does strange things for his son. I believe in law and order, and I hated that you joined those revolutionaries. But I figured out that this might be the only way you could design an escape from them. I even had a fantasy that it was you who blew them all up. So when the police showed me a chunk of a knee that had a crescent-shaped scar on it, I told them that I was sure that was yours—an old football injury. I don't know if they checked your medical records, but they stopped asking me to come in and see what new body part they had found. I hope that I helped you.

There are two sets of circumstances that may be in effect as you read this letter. One: I am handing it to you. In that case I am very willing to answer any questions you may have about it. Two: I have died, and you received this as part of my final papers. I am assuming the second scenario. So there are a few things I need to tell you about me.

The first and most important is that I was very proud of you as my son. Oh, I know we had some bitter phone conversations when you dropped out of school to join those bomb throwers. But you very much pleased me growing up. You were slight, yet you held your own, both on the football team and in ROTC. You were always very clever, and your grades were impressive. You took after me, I'm afraid. You have very little of the gentleness of your mother. But I liked that, too. I only regret that we didn't get a chance to know each other after your twenties.

I too grew up. There is a side of me you never knew, because I had to keep it hidden from view. I did the fatherhood-marriage thing like all my peers. But I had a secret. I love both men and women, and it took twenty years of living a lie before I could make a clean break from the claustrophobic box of that false life I'd created.

I know your generation is more open about homosexuality, but for my generation there was nothing more shameful than harboring those urges. I'd have more respect as a criminal than as a "pervert." But my natural passions and my heart finally could not be denied.

So I came to San Francisco and sowed many oats, "coming out," as they say. Finally, I found a fine man, and we have a lovely relationship.

24

Of course things are never just that simple. There is a woman in my life also, a remarkable girl. As Woody Allen said, "It doubles your chances for a date on Saturday night."

Your mother still does not know. I'm afraid my older male lover would be harder for her to handle than my younger female one. She would somehow take it personally.

I don't know if I passed this gender orientation on to you. I hope this letter may help you with any conflicting emotions you may have discovered within yourself. There is nothing wrong with bisexuality. It is the way we are hardwired from birth. Though, for your sake, I hope it is not your path. There is a lot of heartbreak and abuse in this society for those who love on the fringes. I have been ostracized by both the gay and the straight community. But, in spite of spiteful people, I have had a grand time!

With that off my chest, I don't know what else to write. I hope we're reading this together over a beer. If you are reading this alone, I'm sorry to be dumping it all on you like this. I did my best to be a father to you, and I hope you took some of my better qualities, and avoided some of my worst. Be well, and try to be happy

—Dad

I had no idea how I felt about that letter. I was touched and infuriated. Even in my reaction I could tell his voice was slightly more insightful and compassionate than the father I knew. It made me miss never getting to know this man, who hid his most passionate secret from the world.

I folded the letter and returned it to the envelope. I put it in the glove compartment. Later I might show it to Rose or to Sally, but for now it was my secret.

All the way home I kept thinking about my dad. Just about the time he was writing that letter he was King of the Hill. Lovers of both genders, a lucrative profession, everything going his way. Three years later he would be dead. There's a dagger hanging over our heads on a very thin thread all the time. We just refuse to look up.

I got home and started typing an e-mail to Sally.

Subject: Life's but a walking shadow
From: Warren@Tarotman.info
To: MyRipley@aol.com
Sent from the Internet (details)
Hi Sweetie:
I'm just feeling the fragility of everything right now. I realize that I mostly write to ask you something, or come over because I need something. I'm so busy these days. I don't just stop in, hang out, and tell you how I feel towards you.

Sally, I'd still be on the run, if it weren't for you. I'd be selling used cars in Spokane, or pulling up oil companies' surveying stakes in Alaska. I'd be off gathering another in a long string of adventures. Risking my life, but never risking my heart.

You changed all that. You're the most amazing woman I ever met. The biggest adventure I ever encountered is learning how to love you. Thank you for believing in me. I'll try to deserve you.

Warren

MONDAY, DECEMBER 19

No more will sin and sorrow grow,
Nor thorns infest the ground;
He'll come and make the blessings flow
Far as the curse was found,
Far as the curse was found,
Far as, far as the curse was found.

—"Joy to the World,"
lyrics by Isaac Watts

CHAPTER SIX

They were my own personal Crabbe and Goyle, though I was no Harry Potter! They came at me out of the night. One was a wiry weasel. As he stumbled toward me, blood ran down the bullet hole in his neck and stained his brown camouflage shirt. The other was a big guy, a football tackle dressed in business casual. He had his head grotesquely twisted at an impossible angle. These twin furies had ravaged my dreams all year. This time they had me pinned against the brick wall of a New York townhouse that was burning from the roof down. Help would never get here in time. There was no escape.

That shrill sound wasn't fire trucks, it was my telephone. I sat up. My bedroom was blessedly free from zombies. It was still dark out. The red numerals on the clock on my bedside table read 5:07. This better not be an insurance salesman!

"Dad, Orrin's dead. Someone shot him last night. They found his body in the river. He just washed up on the bank, right under the Big Dipper roller coaster. Dad, I don't know what to do.

Everything's just falling apart. I don't think I can handle very much more."

Crabbe and Goyle didn't look so bad all of a sudden.

"Easy, honey. I know it looks pretty freaky right now. But you're not alone, and we can work everything out. Just take a deep breath and know I'm right here to help."

"How can you even think about helping me? I was such a bitch yesterday. I figured you'd hang up on me. I just didn't know who else to call."

I felt like I was on the suicide hotline.

"Easy, Fran. Hey, forget about yesterday. I know all about making dramatic scenes, I've made plenty in my time. It kind of goes with the territory of life as a manic-depressive." I heard her make a low growl.

"I know you don't like it when I use that term. The good news is that your horrible stormy weather inside is going to change. Guaranteed. As long as you don't kill yourself."

Her voice sounded weak. "I think about doing it."

"Yeah, we all do. I mean I think everybody thinks about throwing off this mortal coil. But folks with our up-and-down swings think about it weekly."

"Daily."

"Yeah, Fran, I know. Hourly sometimes. What do you need right now?"

"I don't know. Nothing I guess."

She was starting to fade on me.

"Really, Fran. I think I need to come on down."

"No, Warren. That's all right. I feel better now. It was good talking with you."

Her voice was neutral. If you didn't know better you'd think

30

she was calming down. But you'd be wrong, dead wrong. She called me at the top of her arc. Now she would just get more and more wooden. Things would stop mattering. It would be harder and harder to care about anything. And it would be easier and easier to think about how to end all this pain. Pretty soon she'd forget why killing herself was a bad idea. I knew this ride all too well.

"Bull, Fran! Look, I don't ask much. Just don't make any decisions for another couple of hours, OK?"

"OK, Dad."

"Do you have a gun in the house?"

"Look, Dad, I know what you're doing. Back off. I'm not going to kill myself, OK? And no, I don't have any guns. Orrin took them all."

Better. She was back to pissed.

"See you in two hours. Be there, you got it?"

"Fuck you. I'll be here, and you won't have to call poison control, don't worry." She hung up on me. Another good sign.

CHAPTER SEVEN

I was way out of my league. A suicidal, maybe homicidal, manic-depressive mom! I didn't have a clue how to help her. Oh sure, I knew how to mess around with medications for a bipolar fifty-six-year-old guy. But with Fran, I had hormones, breast milk, postpartum depression, all kinds of crap to deal with. I needed an expert.

And I just happened to know one: my therapist, Rose Janeworth. Now all I had to do was talk her into getting involved. At 5:14 in the morning. This might be tricky.

One ringie dingie. Two ringie dingies. "Rose, don't hang up! It's me, Warren. I know it's brutally early in the morning, but I need your help. And no, I'm not hallucinating FBI agents this time. It's my daughter, Fran. Her husband took her kid and left her. Then he got shot. Dead. She's lost it, big time."

"Warren . . ."

I interrupted her. Her voice had that this-isn't-worth-a-five-A.M.-call tone to it. I had to entice her; just saving some stranger's life might not be enough.

"Rose, she needs to see somebody right away. I'm worried that she may just kill herself. I'm leaving for Santa Cruz on my bike. I would really love it if you could come along."

This was blatant manipulation. I'd noticed how she would straighten up and lean in a little whenever I mentioned my motorcycle, an Aprilia RSV Mille. It put almost a thousand cc's between your legs and did fifty just sitting in the garage. Once you were on the road the only thing that could beat it was the traffic helicopter. I hoped that somewhere in her checkered past Rose had been a biker bitch.

Long pause.

"Warren, you are a trial. But this does sound like a real emergency. I will come along, but only on one condition."

"Rose, anything!"

"I drive!"

"Wait a minute, Rose. This is no Vespa. Do you think . . ."

"Make no assumptions about me, Warren. I raced Vincent Black Shadows before you were weaned. I'll meet you at Alfredo's."

This was too weird. "How do you know where I keep my bike?"

"Al works on my Suzuki. I've heard you go on for hours about that bike. I've seen your Aprilia parked in the corner of his shop. There can't be more than one of those in Berkeley. See you there in fifteen minutes."

I wasn't too keen on being a passenger. I'd never let anyone drive my bike before. But she had me pinned and wriggling on the wall.

"OK."

Al looked amused as two of his best customers showed up in leathers, ready to ride. But that expression turned into a look of

34

amazement when the older woman got on my bike and cranked her up. He looked at me quizzically.

"Don't ask." I jammed on my helmet and climbed on behind. I don't know why I felt humiliated to have my therapist, practically old enough to be my mother, in command of my bike. Freud would have had a field day.

Once we hit the freeway I stopped worrying about whether or not this was too much bike for her. I leaned with her as she whipped around Peterbilts, cut off SUVs, sashayed past sleepy commuters, toasted the straightaways, and straightened out the curvy pass over the Coastal Range. That woman sure could ride bike.

She pulled over on Ocean Street in Santa Cruz, climbed off, took off her helmet, shook her gray hair, looked at her watch, and laughed. "Berkeley to Santa Cruz in sixty-five minutes. I wouldn't have believed it. Warren, that's the best damn bike I ever drove. Thank God I got the chance to do that once before I died. You can have her back now."

I would never know all the different sides to Rose. I looked at her, eyes sparkling, a grin as wide as the galaxy. I'd never seen her so alive! Hell, we could do this every weekend as far as I was concerned!

CHAPTER EIGHT

Then I looked around us and got the creeps. I don't know why this town does that to me. I should love Santa Cruz. It's a cute, clean, progressive party town. Maybe it's 'cause I'm old. These days I can't do five lines of blow, make a big dent in a pony keg, go ape on the beach volleyball court, and then boogie till dawn. But in spite of the party frenzy, the town always made me a little sad, like somehow it lost itself.

Santa Cruz was in a well-scrubbed depression. Industries already fled from the leftist political takeover. The town's tax base was in the toilet. As the potholes deepened, folks just steered their bicycles around them, smiled, and breathed in the clean air. Everyone looked so wholesome, organic, and healthy, you'd never know that the city was adrift and starving.

Grinning all the way to the slaughterhouse. That was also a little like how I felt right now, on my way toward Fran's. I knew she was a powder keg. She might just throw Rose and me right out on our keisters. Assuming she wasn't lying dead in a pool of vomit. I doubted that anything good was going to come out of this. But I guess this is what dads do. Into the valley of death rode the Big Daddy.

I set a sedate pace as we worked our way across town and north to the Westcliff area. It was one of those rare fogless mornings, complete with gulls crying overhead and a salty onshore breeze. No wonder folks thought this was worth the two-hour commute to Silicon Valley. I wanted to show Rose the scenic route, complete with surfers, fishing boats, and roller coasters. But I imagined us discovering a corpse. So I went direct.

We drove around Walk Circle until I saw Fran's white clapboard cottage, with her red Mini Cooper convertible parked in front. We locked our helmets on the bike and started up the brick pathway through the garden to her front door. Here come two Samaritans in full leather.

Fran materialized akimbo in the doorway; Medusa hair, dark hazel eyes, and furrows in her brow deep enough to plant carrots in. "Who's she?" she demanded.

I had learned in the coffee shop that the nice guy approach didn't work with my daughter. So, what the hell. "Her name is Rose Janeworth. She's a damn good therapist and you're going to talk to her or I'm going to put you over my knee and spank you!"

Fran just shook her head. But she almost smiled.

"OK, Warren, whatever. Come on in, I'll put on another pot of coffee." She turned and we trailed her into the house. "I was getting ready to take a drive. You just caught me."

Manic-depressives don't just take a drive; they take flight. But Rose beat me to it.

"To Las Vegas?" she asked.

Fran stopped dead and turned around slowly. She just stared at Rose.

Rose stared back. "No, Fran, I'm no psychic. I saw the bags by the front door. And if you're anything like Warren, you crave excitement. Vegas tops that chart. It was just a lucky guess."

Fran said nothing, just led us into her kitchen. One point for Rose.

We sat at the kitchen table and waited for stimulants. No one spoke as Fran went through the ritual: grind the beans, boil the water, and fill the Melitta filter with Organic Tanzanian. She was a caffeine connoisseur like her old man. Fran placed the steaming mugs in front of us and sat down with hers. Rose took charge.

"Warren's filled me in about the details of what's going on for you, but I don't know how much of that is just Warren's version, which is often skewed. Why don't you tell me what's really going on, in your own words."

Brilliant. It's the chicks against the stupid guy. Rose knew her stuff.

Fran sighed from her belly. She looked at Rose, and must have liked what she saw, because she launched right in.

"My husband is—I mean *was*—an asshole. We were married a year before Justin was born. As soon as the baby showed up it started to sour. Orrin wanted to hang out with his cop buddies and drink. He wanted his trophy wife quiet and compliant. I'm not good at that.

"Our fights started to get out of hand. He's smaller than me, but he's—I mean, he was ruthless. He was a dirty fighter. Well, when he told me he was taking Justin and moving in with his folks, I lost it. We had one nasty fight after another. Little Justin just sat there and watched his parents scream and hit and threaten each other. Twice the cops showed up. The last time one of them had to sit on me while Orrin took Justin and left."

Rose said, "No justice in this town if you're married to a cop, right?"

"Damn straight."

"So now he's dead."

"Yeah, and they think I did it. I don't have an alibi. I was out drinking. There're a lot of parts of last night I don't even remember. Orrin's ex-partner called me this morning and yelled at me. He told me he'd bust my chops, if it was the last thing he ever did. He was the cop that sat on me when I screamed at Orrin that I wanted to kill him. You know cops, once they decide you're guilty, they stop looking around. They just focus on how to build the case against you—I mean against me. I can't handle it."

Rose said, gently, "You're not alone, Fran. Warren is here, and he brought me down. Are there others in town who could support you in all this?"

"Maybe my minister, Larry Dalton. He's an old friend of Orrin's. But he called me this morning. He'd heard the news, and he was worried about me. That's nice."

Rose said in her firm but caring command tone, "Call him right now, and see if he can come over."

"But it's Monday. He's resting from Sunday service. I can't . . ."

"Call him. He already called you. This is the best part of his job, actually helping out someone in his congregation who is in need. Trust me. Call!"

I've never been able to say no when Rose uses this voice. Fran was no match for her either. She headed for the phone and started to dial.

I bent over toward Rose. "How do you do that? Make people do what you want them to do? Is it witchcraft or something?"

She smiled. "Jedi training. Let the force be with you."

I'm not sure she was kidding.

Fran came back to the table. "He's coming right over. Thanks for your help. You can go now. Everything is under control."

Famous manic-depressive trick. Tell everyone, "I'm fine now. You can go home. Thanks for your help." Then go off and do something incredibly stupid. Rose didn't fall for it.

"Oh, don't worry, Fran. We'll leave soon. But before we go, just sit down for a second. This is excellent coffee, by the way. You're going to have to tell me what blend you use. Now, I'd like to talk with you about some stuff that I think might be able to help you get through the rough spots during these next few weeks."

Rose was easing into the medication discussion, so I got up to wander around. I stopped at the mantel, where there was an empty picture frame. Sure enough, when I squatted down and poked through the ashes I found the edges of a photo. Bet it was of Orrin.

Just then someone started pounding on the front door. I looked out the front window and saw a white police cruiser parked next to my bike. Some days were just more special than other days.

Since there were no flare-ups from the dining room, it looked like Rose was being more effective in talking about mood stabilizers than I had been. I yelled to the gals in the back room, "I'll get it."

CHAPTER NINE

I opened the door and looked up at Conan the Constable. Gray-blond marine haircut, steel gray eyes, dark tan, shoulders an ox would envy, and a triple-x gut. He looked startled. "Who are you?"

"Who are you?" I parried.

He began to walk past me into the house. I took my Aikido "I am an oak tree" energy-grounding stance and he stopped just before running into me.

"Get out of my way!"

I held out my hand, "Cross my palm with a search warrant and you are more than welcome to enter."

He yelled over my shoulder, "Fran, tell this jerk to get out of my way!"

I was thinking about her packed luggage just on the other side of the door. I jumped in before Fran could speak, "Fran, let him in here and anything he sees can be used as evidence."

Fran called out from the kitchen, "Ted, that jerk is my father. Just wait for me on the front porch. I'll be right out."

I smiled, took a step backward, and slammed the door in his face. This was fun.

Fran came up behind me, looking scared. "What should I do?" Rose was by her side.

Back in the sixties, instead of finishing college, I led a revolution. I took Pig Baiting 101. I majored in Managing the Man. I had a Ph.D. in Resisting Police Harassment. This was my turf. "I'll go out there with you. Don't answer any question or make any statement without my OK. Any time you want to, you can just turn around, walk back into the house, and he can't do a damn thing. Let's see what he wants."

She nodded, and I opened the door. Colossus was still rooted there, working up a fine simmer. The three of us walked outside, forcing him to back up.

I led out. "May I see your identification?"

"Step aside buddy, I want to talk with Fran, privately! Fran, tell this guy who I am."

I gave Fran a "wait" hand signal behind my back and said, "Either you show me your identification, or Fran and I turn around and walk back in the house. Then I will call the station to report an officer who refuses to show ID when asked. Your move."

He pulled out his wallet and flipped it open. "Satisfied?"

"Officer Theodore Vespie, do you have a business card?"

"Not for you. Fran, tell this guy to leave us alone."

Fran just shook her head. She learned fast.

I kept it up. "What is your purpose for coming here today?"

"Look, buddy, I can just haul her down to the station if that's what you want."

I was ready for that line. "Why don't you do that? And I will teach her the magic phrase, 'I need to speak with my lawyer.' Then you can ask questions to her mute body all day long."

He was getting very annoyed with me. I, on the other hand, was having a hell of a good time.

He tried to ignore me. "Fran, I need to know where you were last evening."

This was such an irregular interrogation that I began to get a hunch. "You're not assigned to this investigation, are you, Officer Vespie?"

"That's none of your damn business, Mr. Biker. Orrin Wilkins was my partner. And a damn good friend. I know a hell of a lot about your daughter there. Two days ago I was standing right here on this porch when she threatened to kill him. I'm just—wait, Fran, come back here."

I could sense Fran and Rose going back in the house. Good. I kept my focus on Megahunk.

"I don't think Homicide is going to appreciate you butting into their investigation."

Those red blood vessels in his cheeks worked overtime. I wondered if I could get him to punch me. That might help Fran out a lot, if she did end up getting busted for this.

"Look, mister. I don't care if you *are* her father; you're way out of line. You are interfering with the investigation of a crime. I can just haul your sorry ass down to the station and let you cool out behind bars for a while."

What Officer Vespie didn't know was that, behind him, someone in a blue Volvo had just parked behind the squad car. The man who emerged could have been an understudy for the role of Ichabod Crane—tall, pale, angular, and horsy-looking. He wore a knit polo shirt and khaki slacks. The good reverend, was my guess. A witness, how perfect.

"I would very much enjoy slapping a false arrest suit on you. Why don't you try it, Teddy? Maybe we could add aggravated assault."

He took a step forward. This was so old school; I loved it.

"Hello, Ted, how are you doing?"

Sus domesticus swung around to face the newcomer. I watched his shoulder drop, as he saw who it was. Darn. Drama over. He said, "Ah, Reverend. Hi. What are you doing here?"

"I'm here to see Fran, Ted. Am I interfering with anything?"

"No, no. Actually, I was just leaving."

"Ted, are you going to be able to help out at the Casino Night this Saturday? Lorraine is looking forward to you being there."

"Yeah, sure. I already got a sitter for my boy."

"OK, see you then."

Officer Vespie strode to his car, ignoring me completely. Round one to me. I shook hands and introduced myself to my inadvertent rescuer. "Hello. I'm Warren Ritter, Fran's father. You must be Reverend Dalton."

"Hi. You can call me Larry. It's good to meet you, Mr. Ritter. Fran never mentioned that you lived nearby."

No wonder, since we'd only met three times. "And you can call me Warren. I always feel like my old man when someone calls me Mr. Ritter. Come on in."

Fran looked very glad to see him. I actually got to see a whole-face smile, the first one I'd seen on her face since this whole mess began. They started chatting each other up at the kitchen table. Rose pulled me back into the living room.

"Warren, I'm going to stay here awhile. Fran offered to drive me back home. I can set up a med consult when we get to the East Bay and start to get her moods stabilized. The drive up should give the two of us a good time to talk."

"Rose, you're a lifesaver. Is this going to mess up your schedule?"

"I don't see clients on Monday, so this was the perfect time to schedule an emergency."

"I owe you big time!"

"You sure do." She grinned.

I interrupted Larry's pastor-like sounds to tell Fran I was leaving to go find out what, if anything, the police had on her. She jumped up and gave me a genuine full-body hug. That was a first, too.

As I turned onto Ocean Avenue I noticed a white police cruiser right behind me.

CHAPTER TEN

That bastard followed me all the way to the on-ramp to Highway 17. I didn't knock down any yuppies in Birkenstocks, so he had to let me get out of town.

I headed to my Temple of Delphi, which in this millennium was housed in a ranch-style house on ten acres in the hills near Hercules, California, out where the East Bay goes Cowboy.

The particular oracle I was interested in consulting had spiky, streaked hair, walnut eyes, and a smile that made you think of puppies. She was one of the world's top hackers, and also my girlfriend (a quaint term for a fifty-six-year-old man to use). She lived in the boondocks north of Berkeley, with her attack dog, Ripley. She captained a wheelchair basketball team and was the first paraplegic to get accepted into the Urban Search and Rescue Response Task Force Dog and Handler Training Program.

I drove up just as her housemate, Heather Talbridge, aka Heather Wellington, came storming out the front door. As I took off my helmet, I heard the end of her rant.

". . . an emancipated minor, and that means I don't have to answer your nosy questions anymore! See you later!" Solid core doors make a sound like a gunshot when they're slammed.

As this green-eyed fury tromped down the sidewalk I came into her radar. "And don't you say a damn word to me, Warren, if you know what's good for you!"

I just saluted her as she got into her Prius and tried to tear out of there. A silent car that takes ten seconds to get to sixty doesn't lay much scratch. But her point was made. I turned and saw that Sally had opened the door to watch the grand exit. She and her rottweiler, Ripley, were framed in the doorway. Sally nodded toward me and then spun around in her new RGK Hi-Lite titanium wheelchair and went back into the house. This wasn't shaping up to be a Hallmark Holiday Season.

"So, what happened between you and Heather?"

Sally was in front of her desk sorting papers. But I could see the sweat on her forehead, and she panted. She said nothing. Ripley and I watched her intently. Finally, she slammed the pile of papers on the desk and spun around to face me.

"I don't deserve to be treated like that by anyone!" Her brown eyes shimmered with rage.

"What happened?"

"This is my house. I have a right to have a few simple rules respected. *I* invited *her* to stay here. That doesn't mean she can waltz in and out anytime she pleases, have beer busts when I'm away, or exploit me in any way she feels like it!"

My guess was that this was a rather one-sided presentation of the dispute. Sally was enjoying all the delights of raising an older teenage daughter. She'd *just* lost the battle for control, as every parent does. Only she wasn't used to losing. I decided not to point any of this out. Wisdom (and fear of having that fire hose of anger turned on me) guided my next words. I responded the way I imagined Rose would. "That sounds pretty hard. You must be pissed."

"Damn right I'm pissed. If this keeps up she is out of here. I won't have it!"

"Um hum." I was getting good at this therapy stuff.

"And if she tries one of those dramatic exits again I'm going to sic Ripley on her."

I'd already been pinned to the ground once by her rottweiler. I knew this was no idle threat. I didn't know what to say. I was out of correct therapeutic responses. That's why Rose makes the big bucks.

I didn't have to worry. The storm started to clear. Sally looked at me and said, "That was a very sweet e-mail you sent me last night, Warren. Thanks. So, I don't think you came over to watch the bloodletting. What does bring you out here?"

"I need your help."

"Uh-oh. I hate that tone of voice. You know, Warren, I think I'm over helping you. Every time I do, someone tries to kill you."

"No. This time is different. Really!" I filled her in about Fran and the day's events. I ended by saying, "Hell, Sally, I'm not even sure that she didn't plug the bastard. But I've got to find out everything I can about her husband, that pig at the door, well, even Reverend Dalton."

Sally said, "Damn, you think it's so simple. Just go to the hacker and get what you need. Look, I don't even touch law enforcement data banks anymore. Since 9/11 everybody's security has gotten really nasty. I don't want some black van pulling up to haul me off."

She must have seen my expression. Her face softened just a fraction. "I'm sorry. I'm just unloading on you, Warren. It looks like it's been a miserable morning for you, too. Look, I'll see what

I can do. I did a favor for the guy that set up the Web site for the Santa Cruz police. Knowing him, I think I might be able to get a back door into their system."

The next request was even dicier. "Um, while you're doing that back door thing, I might need something else."

Long pause. Finally she said, "Yes?"

I didn't want to dump all the sordid details of my father's love life on her quite yet. "I want to know everything you can find out about my father's death. He lived in San Francisco, and died of a heart attack in 1993. He was married to a woman named Julia Hightower at the time he died. Is that enough information?"

"Depends on what you want." She was looking at me quizzically.

"Look, I promise I'll tell you what this is all about very soon. But bottom line, someone suggested to me there may have been something underhanded about the death. Can you just nose around and see what you can find?"

She was smiling now. "Now, *that* sounds interesting. I love to nose. But I'm going to have to put your projects on hold for an hour or so. Right now I have to get out of here and do a hard spin in my chair for at least five miles. I need to burn off some of my pissed-offness at Heather, or I'm going to start smashing up the china. Contact me in twenty-four, OK?"

We kissed, I scratched Ripley behind the ears, and that was that.

CHAPTER ELEVEN

I took the last bite of one of my favorite gourmet meals (a cheesesteak sandwich, extra peppers, extra onions, and curly fries). Nothing is so difficult in life that the proper addition of greasy steak, fried potatoes, and hot sauce can't make things look a little better.

Then I figured I'd better put my sister in the loop. The last time we chatted on the phone, I hadn't talked with her about Fran because I was freaking out about that encounter in the bookstore. The best rule of thumb I knew for dealing with my sister was let sleeping cobras lie. Since then things had escalated out of control. Tara needed to know.

That started a mild case of indigestion. Someday Sister Snake was going to stop biting me. I'd finally thought of what I wanted for this Christmas: a nice sister. I'll have to send my letter to Santa by express mail.

I called from a phone booth on University, just down from The Cheesesteak Shop.

"Hi Tara, this is Richard." She hated my assumed identity, so I knew better than to use "Warren."

"Yes?" Always so friendly.

"I have something I'd like to talk to you about. Can I come over, or can we meet somewhere?"

"Is this about the Eric bookstore thing? If it is, I'm not interested. I'm sorry I gave you that watch. Dad's dead, and digging around in his ashes isn't going to serve anyone."

"No. This is about Fran. Fran's in a lot of trouble. I know you two are not speaking right now. But her husband took Justin from her, and then got himself killed. Fran's a mess right now. She's also a suspect. I'm trying to help."

"Where's Justin?"

"I think her in-laws have him. I'd appreciate any help you could give me."

"I'll call Fran and see if she will speak to me."

OK, I did my good deed. "Thanks. Bye, then."

"Richard." Her voice was softer. "Thanks for calling me. I know you didn't have to. I appreciate you thinking of me. I care a lot about Justin, and about Fran, though she makes caring about her hard sometimes. Anyway, I know you didn't have to call. Thanks."

That was the most warmth I'd had from my sister since our parents got divorced. I was surprised how much it meant to me. I had to swallow and take a deep breath.

"Yeah, well, Tara, I know I have a lot to make up for. But I also know how much you love Justin. So, don't worry. I'll keep you updated. Look, Fran gets in stormy moods. It sounds like you're in the eye of one right now. But don't worry, I'm not going to let Fran shut you out of Justin's life."

"Right now, you're being the brother I remember. It's been a long time since I could say that. Thanks. Goodnight, Richard."

"Goodnight, Tara."

What the hell. Something good might come out of all this crap.

TUESDAY, DECEMBER 20

Away in a manger, no crib for His bed,
The little Lord Jesus lay down His sweet head;
The stars in the heavens looked down where He lay,
The little Lord Jesus asleep on the hay.

—"Away in the Manger,"
traditional Christmas carol

CHAPTER TWELVE

5:15 A.M. The intercom buzzed. What is this, a remake of *Groundhog Day*? And sure enough, again it was my daughter.

"Dad, come downstairs quick. I need you." Click.

This sounded bad. I jumped into sweats, grabbed my keys, and charged down three flights of stairs. As I rounded the last set, I looked out the tall glass panes in the front doors. No one was in front of the building. But there was something at the foot of the brick steps.

The something was a baby stroller complete with a Buddha/Churchill-looking baby in it. He had a stranglehold around the neck of a furry giraffe, and was equally curious about me. A note was duct-taped onto the stroller's handle. I looked up the road in time to see the back end of a red Mini zoom up the hill. This definitely didn't look good.

I don't know squat about babies. I'd learned about a lot of things during the years I'd been on the run: I fished in Alaska, drove a big rig in Nevada, sold skirts in Nordstrom. Manly things like that. But I'd never held anything that tiny before. Except kittens.

This was definitely not a kitten. I made a wildly intuitive guess that the little booger in front of me was my grandson. I didn't need tarot cards for that. Justin just looked up at me, with this scholarly look. Then he said, "*Bah bah na na?*"

"Yes, I suppose that may be true from where you sit, but I don't have a clue to what you just said."

He held up his toy and said, "*Ga!*"

This was no help. I lifted Justin's very heavy stroller and began the long three-story stair climb up to my apartment. Justin was content to ride like a pasha on his elephant. Thankfully he made no other comments. I was just about to become a pariah to my neighbors in my blissfully children-prohibited apartment house.

I staggered into my apartment and set down the royal carriage. I looked around. Poisons in the kitchen, a surge protector with many wires plugged into it snaking across the floor, spitting iron radiators; this kid would be dead in a week if he stayed here. Justin surveyed his new digs, and then looked back at me with his hazel eyes. My hazel eyes. My grandson. Damn!

I ducked his intent stare and pulled off the note from my generous daughter.

Dear Warren:

Look, I really appreciate all that you've done for me, and now I have to ask you to do even more. I just couldn't leave Justin in that Republican, fundamentalist Christian hell hole of a household any longer. I mean, I'm a Christian, too, but that doesn't mean I have to be a fascist. So I kind of re-kidnapped him from them late last night, while the old farts were asleep.

Anyway, I took him back last night without really thinking about it too much. I left a note that told them I went back east to my mom's. Which I will not do! Then I realized that I can't keep him right now. I'm a mess. The police might arrest me. I don't want them taking my kid away again! So I needed to make him disappear.

That's when I thought of you. You changed your name and disappeared back in the seventies, and no one knew it till now. I figured you must know something about how to hide someone, you're perfect. No one knows about you in my life, except my minister, and he doesn't know very much.

Please call Mom, and Aunt Tara too, I guess, and let them know Justin wasn't kidnapped. I'll come back for him when I can. This way, no matter what happens to me, at least I know that Justin is in the hands of someone who won't judge him, or think he's crazy. Thanks Dad, I can't tell you how much this means to me.

Your daughter, Francine

Oh, my God! I needed to let Justin know the score. "Look, Justin, this is nuts! I know you don't know very much about how things are supposed to go, but let me assure you this is way out of the box. You know, I gotta tell you I'm getting a little pissed at all the crap that keeps flying in my direction."

Justin looked like he was considering what I just told him. He had a studious look on his face. Then his forehead wrinkled just about the same time the smell hit me. He had other things on his mind besides my whining.

What the hell was I supposed to do now? Man, that poop stunk. I didn't know how to do these things! Double damn. I unbelted him and lifted him out of his stroller. Wow, he sure was light. But proximity didn't make that smell any better. He was wearing some sort of plastic-paper thing, stuck on with adhesive tabs. I held him out in front of me and prayed that those diapers were leak-proof. They looked good for now, so I put him over my shoulder. I grabbed a towel from the bathroom and tossed it on my bed.

The second I tipped Grandpa's Favorite on his back, he began to cry. Oh boy, here comes the eviction notice. I frantically ripped at the adhesive tabs and the whole diaper thing opened up in all its anal splendor before me. The entire experience of dirty bottom, gooey poop, and asphyxiating smell made me want to gag. I don't get it. What keeps mothers from just tossing the baby in the diaper pail and keeping all those sweet-smelling, clean diapers uncorrupted? I grabbed the sack of fecal matter and dumped it on the floor. Hardwood. It cleans pretty well.

Well, no one was going to save me from this. I had to find some way to silence the howler monkey. I handed him his giraffe, after ripping off the plastic thread that attached the price tag from a toy store. Ouch, those things hurt. No luck. Justin grabbed the stuffed animal but kept on crying.

I looked back at that millstone of a stroller. Now I noticed the zipped up, bulging rear compartment. I watched Justin, but he wasn't jumping up or down or flying or anything, so I hoped he would stay put. I ran over and unzipped the pocket. Tons of packages of incomprehensible stuff erupted. But one of them was marked LUVS ULTRA LEAKGUARDS and another was marked BERKLEY & JENSEN UNSCENTED BABY WIPES. Now we're talking!

I ripped open those wipes things and pulled one out. Then I had to touch the smeary backside of my little critter. God, this was so gross! I wiped him off and dropped the soiled wipes on top of the ex-diaper. Could I get diseases from all this?

I opened one of the Luvs. OK, it looked pretty simple. Thank God for no pins! I plunked Justin on the middle of all that paper and plastic and taped up all the edges I could find. He rewarded me with a succinct "*Sha*," which I think was a compliment. Then his forehead started to wrinkle, like he was winding up for another howl.

I lobbed the giraffe into his lap, but that didn't seem to do the trick. Back to the treasures in the perambulator. Sure enough there was a Ziploc bag that contained a bottle. After I inserted the nipple into Justin's mouth, peace once again returned.

I noticed a plastic bottle labeled Similac Advance Infant Formula, so I guess we were well stocked to create the next messy diaper. I gingerly picked up the paper mess on my floor and zipped it closed in a Hefty freezer bag. Ah, the odor was finally contained! Parenthood is an anxiety-producing, exhausting enterprise, and I had only been at it for about ten minutes. I'd never make it through the day. Time for reinforcements!

CHAPTER THIRTEEN

The first call was to Fran's cell phone. I got, "I'm not answering calls right now. Leave your number, even if you think I know it, and I'll get back someday. Beep."

"Fran, call me. It's Warren." Then I gave her my goddamn number.

I had better luck with the second call.

Sally's voice was a little rusty. "A little early, isn't it, Warren?"

"Not too early for the five-month-old boy nursing on my bed."

"Excuse me?"

"My whacked-out daughter left him on my doorstep. I even had to change his diapers. Disgusting! Sally, I need your help!"

Her raucous laughter didn't help any. She finally pulled herself together and said, "How do you do it, Warren? OK, bring your little bambino on over and we'll see what we can do. Do you have a car seat?"

Sure my car had seats. Then I realized she meant one for Justin.

I looked at the stroller. Sure enough, the seat part looked detachable. "I think so. Thanks, Sally, I really need some help here!"

I lugged the 150-pound carrier and the fifteen-pound boy down three flights, praying for my landlord to sleep in. One Asian girl came down the hallway and stared at me, like I was smuggling bales of marijuana or something. What, she's never seen a fifty-six-year-old single guy with a baby before?

Sally greeted me in the driveway, and took Justin out of my hands. She did the usual googly goo things that women do with babies. Where do they learn this stuff?

Justin looked quite pleased to receive this primitive level of communication. He laughed as Ripley licked him. Then Sally showed me how to hold him to protect his neck. I slung him back over my shoulder, set up the stroller, and we wheeled into her house.

I looked around at her floors, equally littered with electrical cords and other lethal baby traps. "Do you think it's safe to put him down?"

"Unless he's allergic to dog hair. Warren, he won't crawl around for a few more months, don't worry."

How was I supposed to know that? I plunked Justin down on a rug. Sally pointed and said, "Af!" and Ripley lay down beside him, which pleased Justin greatly, if that is what "*Ba, ba, ba*" means. Justin and Ripley began chewing on different ends of Justin's giraffe.

"Where's Heather?"

The smile faded. "Well, you're the un-father of a baby, and I'm the un-mother of a teenager who didn't come home last night."

"You know, Sally, we're going to need her help for this baby thing."

"What do you mean 'this baby thing'? I'm not taking a baby in here, that's for sure!"

I was desperate. "Look, Sally, I didn't start this, so don't give me that stinky-eye look. I can't have him in my apartment. I don't know what to do. What if Fran doesn't come back? I don't want to get picked up for kidnapping."

An unhealthy silence descended, punctuated only by an occasional "*Ga*."

Finally a sigh of resignation from Sally. "OK, Warren, you're right. We do need Heather, for babysitting if for nothing else. Don't worry about kidnapping. I'm sure you can get one of your friends to mock up a convincing birth certificate. I can get a phony birth record put into the files at Berkeley General. I can't get into Social Security Administration, so the ID won't hold up for too long."

"It's good enough."

"In a day you will become an instant dad, until Fran comes back to claim Justin."

"Just what I always wanted. Not."

Sally got on the phone to Heather's boyfriend's mother and began to try to track Heather down. I made a call to the cell phone of a low-life forger I knew and confirmed the price for a local birth certificate. I heard Sally talking with Heather, and started to relax when I heard her laugh.

I called Rose and got her voice mail. "Well, Rosie, I guess those meds you got Fran haven't quite kicked in yet. She swiped her son from her in-laws last night, dropped him on my doorstep very early this morning, and now she's disappeared. Remind you of anyone? Blood breeds true. You might want to see if you can have a few words with her today."

Sally went into the kitchen, and soon the two of us were settled in front of the fireplace, sipping fruit smoothies and watching Justin chew on his foot.

Sally looked up from this bucolic scene and said, "What kind of mother would do this to her child?"

"A desperate, mentally ill mom who loves her kid a whole lot. I might have done the same thing. I'm only beginning to understand my dad, but I think he might have had the same bipolar curse that Fran and I have. When he split, Mom treated me like a member of an exotic, sharp-toothed species, someone she only wanted to watch from afar. I'm betting Cathy, Fran's mom, felt the same way."

"Fran didn't want Justin to get the same zookeeper treatment. She knew that those in-laws would end up making Justin feel crazy. She can't be a parent herself right now; she's got her work cut out for her just trying to contain her internal tornado. But she's doing what she can for Justin."

"Maybe, but he's only five months old, for Christ's sake. His only mood swings come from dirty diapers."

"Hey, remember the 'mentally ill' part? I'm not saying she's in contention for the Sanest Mom of the Year Award."

Sally said, "You're right, Warren. I can't understand it. But I'll believe you. Anyway, while I was up waiting all night for Heather to come home, I made some progress on the stuff you gave me.

"First thing, I don't see anything unusual about your dad's death. Straightforward heart attack, complete with a statement of pre-existing cardiac conditions confirmed by his personal physician. Nothing out of order. Here's a copy of the death certificate. I'll poke around a little more but this looks legit."

I took the paper she handed me. I admit I felt a little relieved. Bookstore Eric was just another nutcase.

"Now on the Fran front we made some progress. Your Officer Vespie is in a little hot water. There's a note in his jacket that a file has been opened with the Professional Standards Unit, otherwise known as Internal Affairs. That unit's data is kept offline, so I can't find out any more about their investigation. Those IA units usually keep all their data in computers that never get networked and never get hooked into the Internet. After all, they're going after smart, sneaky cops.

"The deceased, Orrin Wilkins, used to be Vespie's partner, but three months ago Wilkins went on loan to San Jose Police as a part of an investigation coordinated by Homeland Security. He'd gone undercover to join a local anti-war group. I'm scared to touch anything federal anymore, but I was lucky to find a memo in his Santa Cruz file about the assignment. It mentioned the name of the group: the South Bay Force for Freedom. I Googled them and found out they've been meeting the third Tuesday of every month since 1999. Here's the address."

She handed me a copy of their home page. The red, white, and blue banner across the top proclaimed, "Support our Troops. Bring them Home!"

I said, "They're meeting tonight."

"Yep, but you might be occupied elsewhere. Here is the real juicy nugget I unearthed. It seems Fran's good reverend isn't all that good. He has a bit of a record. He was arrested for assault down in Hollywood five years ago. Charges were later dropped, but I've kept a back door open into the LAPD system, and here's the sheet on it, victim's information included. I've verified that Dean Pak is still at that address."

Just then Ripley stood up, the front door burst open, and Heather swooped in. She carried two shopping bags. I could see a jumbo box of Pampers sticking out of the top of one of the bags. "Where's the peach fuzzer?" She saw Justin and the two bags hit the floor. No glass-breaking sounds. "What a sweetie!"

Justin was just as pleased to replace Ripley with Heather, who was even better at the googly goo thing. After extracting a bushel of giggles from the tot, Heather turned to us and said, "I like this little wombat. Warren, it's Christmas. Can I have him?"

CHAPTER FOURTEEN

I left the girls to their ersatz motherhood thing. I had an investigation to work on. I was going down to Tinseltown. I was on my way to the Day-of-the-Locust land. Next stop, Hollywood: the home of Botoxed foreheads, chemical tans, and anorexia. Southwest's flying taxis would get me there in an hour, give or take a few days trying to get through security. I'd like to see Santa Claus try to make it through an airport security checkpoint. He'd lose a few ho, ho, ho's, that's for damn sure. I'd been up six hours already and I still needed caffeine, which wasn't coming anytime soon, from the looks of this line. The headache was about to bring me to my knees.

I'd already stowed all my knives, ice picks, and razor blades in my glove compartment. I breezed through the cavity search and threw myself on the mercy of the nearest Starbucks. I know, I know, "Friends don't let friends go to Starbucks." But I was a desperate and dangerous man. I chugged the triple latte and wolfed down the ham croissant sandwich. That began to take my edge off. One more latte and I'd be ready to contemplate my mission.

I'd bumbled through a couple of earlier investigations this year, I was ready this time. Last month I'd read *The Complete Idiot's Guide to Private Investigating,* and I knew just what to do. Well, sort of. Be prepared (I had Sally's notes), establish trust, talk about what interests the witness, and get him to like you. Look out, Dean, here I come!

Most of Southern California looks like it was built by one architect with a big Xerox machine. But Hollywood still managed to hold on to some of the older stucco homes from a more graceful time, when men played tennis in long pants, and the more daring women were wearing sandals. Dean Pak did not live in one of these.

Driving my rented Kia Rio down North Las Palmas, I was engulfed in apartment buildings. This was one of the most crowded neighborhoods in the U.S. There were plenty of gift shops, bars, and tour buses to make sure you didn't forget that you were steps away from the Hollywood Walk of Fame. I stopped in front of a six-story box. Its name, Estrella Apartments, was painted in light gray. The letters were fading into the once-pink walls.

I pushed the button for number twelve and a tinny, irritated voice came out of the speaker. "Who is it?"

"My name is Warren Ritter. I'm doing a piece on Larry Dalton, and I really need your help."

"Larry, wow. How did you get my name?"

My detective training taught me that if you don't have a good answer, go somewhere else. "I understand the two of you had a falling-out."

Laughter. Then, "You might call it that."

"You are in a unique position to give me information I can't get anywhere else. Can I come up and talk with you? It won't take long, I promise!"

"Completely off the record, and I mean completely!"

"Absolutely! That's not a problem. Your privacy will be completely respected."

I heard the click. I was in.

Knobby gray carpet, a very tired potted palm, piss-yellow walls, and an elevator with an OUT OF ORDER sign on it. I took the stairs to the second floor and knocked on Twelve.

Dean was my height and build, which is to say a little bigger than one of Santa's elves. He'd done a lot more upper body work than I had, but neither of us were going to make you cross the street to get out of our way. He was crisply ironed and in autumn colors. His young Asian face didn't match the lines in his hand as he shook mine, and I guessed him to be closer to fifty than twenty. Microdermabrasion is a miracle worker.

I handed him a bogus business card from the *North Bay Sentinel*, "News for the Rest of Us," with phone numbers and e-mail accounts that Sally had mocked up.

"Come on in. Can I get you a soft drink or a glass of Chablis or something?"

My gaydar was on full alert. He was lightly cruising me. I should have been flattered. These days I don't get cruised much. When I first moved to the Bay Area in the seventies, I had been naively surprised at how friendly guys were toward me. But those days were over. Old guys get ignored.

Before I met Eric I would have had the usual covertly homophobic judgments about this guy's trim clothes and what I could see of the nicely decked-out apartment behind him. But knowing

Dad was in the same fraternity made me feel warmer toward Dean. A little guilty about conning him, too. Weird, huh?

Anyway, no wine for me. I was on a new medication my shrink wanted to try out. I think the protocol goes: Test on amoebas, rabbits, monkeys, and then Warren. After that we'll decide if it's safe for human consumption. Actually the drug wasn't new, it was Dilantin, like folks take for seizures. The big pharmaceuticals were opposed to using it for us bipolars, because we could buy it generic. No big bucks for them in that. Anyway, the stuff was working pretty good, and I didn't want to mess with it. And believe me, alcohol messes with any bipolar medication! "Ice water would be great."

"Pellegrino OK?"

"Perfect."

His taste was refined. I walked around looking at the nicely framed prints by Whatmore, Gockel, and Salinas, and even an etching by Alligand. Finally I sat on his butter yellow leather couch and sighed. Why can't straight guys have a decent aesthetic sense?

He handed me a crystal goblet of water. I took a sip and bet to myself he'd even used bottled water to make the ice cubes. "Excellent, thank you. And I love your taste in modern art. Is that an original Alligand?"

"Yes, do you know him?"

Thank God I wander into the Reprint Mint on a regular basis. "I love some of his new mixed media work."

I passed the test. He set his goblet of Chablis on the glass coffee table and sat next to me. "You're welcome for the water. I noticed you didn't answer my question. How did you get my name?"

Improvise, improvise! "A source who would prefer to remain

anonymous gave it to me. You see, I do keep things confidential if I am asked to."

"I am glad to hear that. And please do the same with what I say to you." He crossed his straight creases, leaned back, and smiled. "OK, fire away."

He was darn cute. I could appreciate his presentation in an abstract way.

"Thanks. Is it OK to call you Dean?"

"I'd prefer it, Warren."

We were getting so friendly. "Well, Dean, I'll tell you what I know and then we can flesh it out together." Hey, I'm not above flirting a little to get what I need. My father's son, after all.

"Lovely."

"Five years ago you and Larry were . . . friends, and one night he got mad at you and hit you. You later dropped the assault charges. Am I somewhere in the ballpark of what really happened?"

"You're standing on home plate."

"How did you two get together?"

"I like white guys, he liked Asians. What do you prefer?" I swear he almost fluttered his long eyelashes. I could have said, "Breasts and wheels," but it would be too hard to explain.

"I like them with opposable thumbs. I hear Larry has a bit of a temper." Very smooth segue. I was totally fishing, and desperately wanting to switch the track of this conversation.

"Larry is one of the nicest guys you'll ever meet. He was going to seminary when we were together, and was just 100 percent sweet. In front of others. But every so often he would get these really dark moods. I usually stayed away from him on those days. I'd already gotten smacked once by him. He was in one of those moods on the day he beat me up. I just picked the wrong time to bicker with him. Unfortunately our door was open and a neighbor called the cops. He left my face a mess, and the police hauled him away before I could stop them. That's the story."

"If you don't mind my asking, what happened between the two of you after that?"

"Oh, I don't mind. He dumped me right after that. I think it made him feel guilty to see my arm in a cast like that. I knew it was partly my fault, but he didn't want any part of me. He transferred to the Ohio campus and I never heard from him again. Do you know where he is now?"

I wasn't going to lie. "Yes. Do you want to know?"

"No, I guess not. Water under the bridge and all that. Speaking of which, would you like another Pellegrino?"

It was time to pull a Colombo. "No, I've got to run. Just one more question, though. Do you think he is capable of killing someone?"

"Larry? No! Well . . . maybe. But he'd have to be really mad at the guy."

CHAPTER FIFTEEN

I still had "miles to go before I sleep." Time to become a political activist, something much closer to my heart than pretending to be a reporter.

I flew back to S.F. Then I got in my Civic and headed down to San Jose. I knew the minute I crossed the invisible barrier into the Willow Glen district. Here Christmas was a virus more virulent than Dutch Elm disease. Actually kind of the exact opposite of Dutch Elm disease. Every house had a decorated tree in the front yard. It was weird. I expected to see Cindy-Lou Who any minute.

I found my destination, a pseudocolonial in pale green with rose shutters. Shutters in a climate that rarely saw freezing. There was a peace flag on a stake stuck in the lawn, next to a tree with blue and silver balls on it, and topped with a radiant Star of David. This must be the place.

I used the heavy brass knocker and the door was opened by a six foot six fullback, who more or less expanded out to the door jamb. It was Officer Vespie's peacenik big brother. I felt like Jack at the top of the beanstalk. Instead of "Fee, fie, foe," the giant said, "Who are you?"

"Um, I'm here for the South Bay Force for Freedom meeting."

"We don't know you."

The giant moved to one side when an oddly familiar-looking black man, obviously in charge, put a hand on King Kong's shoulder. "Who do we have here, Jim? What's your name?"

"Warren Ritter. I read about your Tuesday meetings from your Web site, and I thought I'd come over and check them out."

"Well, we've been having a little problem with unwanted Homeland Security interlopers lately."

Damn, I had to get in here, but I had to look like I didn't care. I laughed. "Well, you sure don't have to worry about me in that regard. Look, I live in Berkeley. I was just down in San Jose for the day, and I wanted to see what you folks were doing down here. If it's an inconvenience I'll come back another time."

"Maybe that might be a good idea. This week we are all a little sensitive to strangers."

I knew this guy. I knew his voice, his sloping shoulders. I just didn't know all those wrinkles. I applied mental Botox, and then I had it. I wiggled my finger for him to come closer. The Jolly Green Jim moved back. I whispered, "Hello Levar, it's Traveler." I knew him as Levar Walters or Lebna Wekesa back when he was in the Panthers and I was Traveler, a leader in the Weather Underground.

Weather had a safe house in Chicago two blocks from the Black Panther headquarters. There was a real love-hate relationship between our two organizations. We admired the Panthers, and were doing all we could to support them in leading the revolution to overthrow our corrupt capitalist government. The Panthers were embarrassed by this fawning group of white bomb-throwers. They kept disassociating their community-building efforts from our destructive antics.

But no one was going to tell Levar who he could be friends with. He and I managed to hack out a decent friendship in spite of the racial tension around us. It mostly consisted of shooting pool and drinking beer at a bar halfway between our two headquarters. I think he liked my acerbic sense of humor. I liked his intelligence and his calmness. After 1970 I never expected to see him again.

He looked like he never expected to see me again either. He examined me carefully, and then smiled. This is reunion year for me, and here was yet another link to my nefarious past. This link, however, I didn't need to worry about.

"Traveler? So it is. Well, you are one person I surely don't need to worry about. Come on in, but be damn cool."

"You, too. I'm in no place to be outed."

"Lawrence" introduced me as an old friend and fellow activist to the gathering in the living room. All I had to say is that I worked on Telegraph Avenue, and all the white faces welcomed me without hesitation. The first topic on everybody's mind was Oscar Walker, aka the late Orrin Wilkins. I saw several copies of the San Jose *Mercury News* open to the article with Orrin's picture in it.

Ms. Straight-gray-hair-over-the-shoulders said, "He was so friendly and helpful. And he was so passionate about the spread of the American Empire. I can't believe he was undercover, spoofing us the whole time. What a rat!"

Mr. Balding-golf-shirt-and-slacks chimed in, "He never would invite me over to his place after the meetings. We went out for a couple of drinks, but that was that. I just figured he was private."

The giant snorted, "Yeah, private like the CIA. This friggin' country. What do they think; we're going to bomb Safeway or the golf course or something?"

Tank-girl-in-shorts jumped in, "I don't wish death on anyone. That's what we're all about here. But I might make an exception for traitors like Mr. Walker."

Levar/Lawrence ended the discussion. "Oscar, or Orrin, which was his real name, betrayed us all. He played us and would have tried to destroy us. We're damn lucky some good American put a bullet in his head.

"That's why we need to make sure we vet new members from now on. No one comes in unless one of us knows them. And be aware that the government of the United States is very interested in what goes on in these meetings. I think we should be flattered. If they only knew! Our biggest threat to the American way is the amount of organic ingredients we cram into those cookies."

Folks laughed. Then, I sat through a rather boring meeting about mobilizing for an anti-war rally on January 2. Got to tell you, infiltrating this group was a big waste of taxpayers' time. They were about as revolutionary as that infamous ex-con Martha Stewart. The trail mix cookies and fruit-cheese plate, however, were exceptional, and made an excellent substitute for dinner. Levar and I kept checking each other out. What was he doing in this well-heeled, white bread world? Of course he was probably wondering the same thing about me.

The meeting degenerated into neighborhood chat. I got up and made an exit speech about what a lovely time I had, and what a glowing report I would give to the activists up north. Levar walked me to the door, and then followed me outside and closed the door behind him.

"Well, that was a lot of bull pucky you just dished out. What are you really doing here, Traveler?"

"Look, I'm Warren, and you're Lawrence, right?"

"Absolutely, Mr. Ritter. Now tell me why you're here."

"Long story. Very long story. Can I ask you a question first?"

"Fire away."

"How well did you know Oscar?"

"No dice. We need to talk, and not out here."

"Tomorrow lunch?"

He smiled. "Come over to Mountain View. There's a damn fine pool hall with pretty good bar food. I'd love to wipe you off the table, just for old times' sake." We agreed to meet at the West Coast Snooker and Billiards Club at noon.

It had been a long day, and I was on empty. I had the windows wide open and rock and roll blasting, just to keep my eyes open all the way back home. I was too tired to talk with Sally so I sent her off this e-mail and then crashed.

```
Subject: Bushed!
From: Warren@Tarotman.info
To: MyRipley@aol.com
Sent from the Internet (details)
Hi Sweetie:
Checked out Dean. I'll tell you about it later.
I will pick up J's docs tomorrow. Hope J isn't
driving you both crazy. Orrin's undercover name
was Oscar Walker. You might want to check that
```

out. Also, I need you to check out Lawrence
West aka Lebna Wekesa and Levar Walters. South
Bay. He was at that meeting you sent me to.
Very confidential, please, he's a friend.

   Night.

                                        Warren

WEDNESDAY, DECEMBER 21

O ye, beneath life's crushing load
Whose forms are bending low,
Who toil along the climbing way
With painful steps and slow;
Look now! for glad and golden hours
Come swiftly on the wing;
O rest beside the weary road
And hear the angels sing.

—"It Came Upon a Midnight Clear,"
Edmund H. Sears

CHAPTER SIXTEEN

Warren Ritter."

I looked up from my morning latte and *Chronicle* into the ice blue eyes of one of my least favorite people, Special Agent David Stiles, with the Federal Bureau of Investigation. Agent Stiles had tried to hang a murder/kidnapping on me.

He was a grown-up Aryan Youth on steroids. He stood, casually overdressed, in double-pleated, slash-pocketed wool slacks that hung like they were cut to him, a gray cashmere two-button blazer with side vents, and those Italian loafers with dangly cross-strap tassels. (I take notice of clothes that cost as much as a down payment on an SUV.) He was either a rich kid playing cop, or a Saudi infiltrator with really good makeup.

"Davie, I see California is getting to you. You ditched the navy suit with the understated red power tie."

"Hello, Mr. Ritter. May I sit down?"

To answer honestly and tell him to bugger off would only make things worse. Earlier this year he searched my place, staked out my apartment building, and confiscated my car. I had no doubt this man could make this Christmas much worse.

We were in the Med, the same coffee shop where I'd had that disastrous conversation with my daughter just three days earlier. The room was full of caffeine junkies who appeared to read their *New York Times* while covertly checking out the cop who looked like he just stepped out of *Esquire*.

"Please, Agent Stiles, have a seat. How can I help you? Let's see, the last time I asked you that, you ended up trying to arrest me. I can't wait to see what happens this time."

"And I'm very glad to see you again, Mr. Ritter. I was never satisfied at how that whole kidnapping affair turned out. A little too convenient for you, in my opinion. Therefore imagine my surprise in this morning's surveillance briefing when I saw your face in one of the photographs. What were you doing at the South Bay Force for Freedom meeting last night?"

"Exercising my constitutional right to peacefully gather and assemble to support or oppose a public policy. I think that's also an exercise of my right to free speech. Do you have a problem with those constitutionally guaranteed rights?"

"If you're running for the Supreme Court you have a long road ahead of you. What's your connection with that organization?"

"You know, Dave, I'm a law-abiding citizen. I pay my taxes, which help pay your salary, by the way, and I don't get even so much as a parking ticket. So why are you sitting here asking me these questions?"

"I don't need to justify my actions to you. I will tell you, however, that this particular organization has come under the attention of Homeland Security as one with possible connections to terrorist groups outside the United States."

I took another sip of my latte. "Was it the trail mix cookies that tipped you off, or was it that your spy, Oscar Walker, got shot?"

"How do you know about that?"

"It was the number one agenda for last night's group. They read the newspapers, too. They spent the evening talking about it. They never got around to discussing their plans to hijack a Greyhound bus and crash it into the J. Edgar Hoover Building."

"What plans?"

I rubbed my eyes. Dudley Do-Right was just too dense. "That was a feeble attempt at a joke, Dave."

"A man died. And terrorists attacked our nation. Every day we are fighting a war on terror, to keep this country and this world free. Those things are not material for jokes."

"Oh yeah? Well, what about Bill Maher's joke: the one about Condi Rice. Remember when she testified to Congress that the whole debacle about weapons of mass destruction was because of 'flawed intelligence'? Well, that afternoon Bush calls her in his office and says, 'You weren't talking about me, were you?' Come on, that's pretty funny."

Not the slightest trace of a grin. Oh, well.

Instead Dave said, "We need to know exactly who was in that meeting and what transpired. First of all, what were you doing there?"

"Oh, I see those folks all the time at peace rallies. They'd invited me to come down and chat with them. I happened to be in the neighborhood, so I dropped in."

"Which peace rallies?"

"You do not have a need to know that. Besides, just check your pictures. I'm sure you'll recognize me."

He was getting pissed. I have that effect on law enforcement. I don't know why. I try so hard to please.

"Why were you in the neighborhood last night?"

"Visiting a sick relative, and don't bother asking, because I'm not going to give you that information either."

"Who do you know in the South Bay Force for Freedom?"

"Jim, what's his name, the really big guy. That's the only name I can remember."

"I find that hard to believe."

"It's a congenital thing, Dan—oh, I mean Dave. See what I mean?"

"Just answer my questions."

I'd had enough. "Dave, either toss me in the black van and drive me off to Guantanamo Bay, or let's finish up here. I have an appointment in just a few minutes. And look, here's the thing. Now that I know you're watching that group, I'm staying far away from it. I don't want to get anywhere near one of your investigations, I assure you!"

This was the first thing I'd said that seemed to please him. "I'm glad to hear that, Mr. Ritter. If you stay away from that organization we may not need to extend our investigation to you. However, I want you to keep our conversation in strictest secrecy."

"Look, I guarantee that I will avoid the whole group like the plague. You can trust me on that. And I'd be the last person to tell them that I talked with the FBI. My lips are sealed."

As he walked away I uncrossed my fingers.

CHAPTER SEVENTEEN

I needed to get some of that federal pollution out of my aura. I decided to check in with Sally. She picked up right away.

"Warren?"

"Hi, doll. I just finished chatting with my favorite Fed, and thought I'd like to talk with a real person."

"You're on your cell aren't you?"

"Um, yes."

"Don't do that. Anyone can listen in. Go call me on a land line. I have some not-so-happy information for you. Later." Oops, my mistake.

It was an easy downhill stroll to the pay phones by Andronaco's. There wasn't a cloud in the sky. But inside was stormy weather. I had a stratocumulus bouncing around in my head. What did she mean by not-so-happy information?

"Hi, it's me again."

"Better. You know, Warren, sometimes I'm amazed that you stayed undercover for so long."

"Me and Osama."

"Goofball. Anyway there *is* something fishy about your dad's death: his second wife. Julia Hightower only exists from the age of eighteen on. There's no birth record, no school record, nada until she shows up as a freshman at UCLA, where she enrolled as a California resident. I have a darn good database for California, and this is weird. She seems to have sprung up from the earth as a mature teenager. Rather odd, don't you think?"

"Go get her, Sally. Do you need me to go down and check out UCLA?"

Sally sighed. "You couldn't do anything unless you were a cop with a court order. They're getting really tight about student files. No, I'll go picking around at Julia some more. You stir up some clues. Mmumph, somebody just stuck a giraffe in my mouth. You go have a great day, Warren. I'm lying around with the kid for a while."

"Give him a kiss from me. We'll talk later, sweetie."

CHAPTER EIGHTEEN

This is top-quality work. The signature is perfect; the stamp has the same imperfections as the real thing. Of course the tiny fingerprints are different. I got these off of my niece's little girl. What an adorable cannoli she is! So, except for the prints, this gorgeous piece could stand up in court! And done in less than twenty-four hours! Four hundred dollars, please."

"Joey, you are a master." As I counted out my Franklins, Joey sat back and rested his precious hands on his balloon of a stomach. He was a bulbous guy, with tiny, elegant, and very steady hands.

Anyone with as many identities as I had needed to know a good forger. I met him through Alfredo, my motorcycle mechanic. Al's uncle was a mechanic in the underworld sense of the word: a hit man for the Mafia. So Al knew the best in the Bay Area for what I needed. Joey was fast, accurate, and very expensive.

The birth certificate for Justin Ritter *was* a work of genius. It was a little roughed up as though it had been handled a lot in the past five months. Justin's poor mother died in childbirth, but his brave dad, yours truly, was raising him alone. I hoped this wasn't an omen. Anyway, as long as no one checked the fingerprints on the certificate against Justin's, he was now officially mine. Goodie.

"Hey, tell your girlfriend, Sally, if she ever wants to work with a partner, there's a big need out there for these. She could do the data, I could do the documents. We could clean up!"

"She tends to want to work alone, but I'll pass it along. Thanks, again, Joey."

I closed the door as he called out to me, "Russian orphans. A really big market these days!"

CHAPTER NINETEEN

The sign over the door read, *Epic Thrash: A Bike Shop for the X-tremely Demented!* My only male friend was a bike cop in Berkeley, Jim McNally. Or he had been. As far as the Berkeley Police Department knew, he went on unpaid leave for a month while he was getting over the effects of being run over by an SUV. In truth he'd used that time to open a boutique bike shop in Hayward for fanatical cross-country maniacs who wanted to kill themselves on absolutely state-of-the-art equipment. Now he was holding down two jobs. Once he actually started making money in retail, his resignation letter would hit his sergeant's desk.

I walked into the tiny shop on Main Street. Frames and wheels hung from the walls and the ceilings. A glass display counter ran down one side, crammed full of derailleurs, brakes, and God knows what all. Mac stood at a workbench in the middle of the room doing something to the spokes of a wheel.

He looked up and grinned, "Hey Warren, look at these: Campy

Stheno rims, with polycentric slanted sidewalls, a Hugi 240 hub and Ritchey Logic spokes! This wheel rocks!"

I had no idea what language he was using, so I said, "Cool! Looks like you got an order."

He put down the little thingie he was using and came over and gave me a high five. "A sweet six-thousand-dollar bike. And more on the way. I'm turning in my letter next week! Tell your investor I am ready for Phase Three."

I'd convinced Mac that I was the go-between for a rich client of mine. Actually it was my dough bankrolling his escape from law enforcement, but I didn't want anyone to know how much money I had tucked away in my Microsoft stock nest egg.

I'd come just in time. He was just about to become useless as a source of cop talk. "I'll pass on the word, Mac. But I have a favor to ask in return. I need the scoop on two Santa Cruz cops, one living and one not."

"You're messing around with another murder, aren't you?"

"Well, yes. But I can't tell you too much about it. You've got to take my word on this, it's very personal."

A sigh. "You're incorrigible. But I'll give you anything I can. I'll call around. I can talk to Sam. I went through the Academy with him. He works the bike squad in Santa Cruz. So who are the guys you want information about?"

CHAPTER TWENTY

The cue ball banked off the rail and just tipped the eight ball before running out of steam. But a tip was all that was needed, as the black ball dropped over the lip and disappeared into the corner pocket.

"That's five straight, Warren, want to try for an even six-pack?"

I'd forgotten that Levar/Lawrence was a shark. He could give me a five-ball handicap and still run me off the table. This was less than fun.

"I should have known I was in trouble when you pulled out your membership card. Let's go try out those cheeseburgers. I need to talk with you, which has to be far more entertaining than watching you humiliate me."

"Too bad, I think your luck was just about to change."

"It already has; we're halfway to the bar."

I had already briefed Levar about my chat with Special Agent Dave. We'd talked in my car before I went into the pool hall to be humiliated by him. Levar wasn't surprised to find out that the meeting was under surveillance. I suggested that they go over to the van that was staking out their meeting, and invite the agents in for some of those brownies and a little chat about the role of the FBI in taking away the rights of United States citizens. He loved the idea.

The agony of defeat slowly ebbed once I had a plate in front of me with a rare burger, oozing cheddar cheese and surrounded by a mountain range of crispy fries. All conversation ceased. More important things faced us, like disproving once and for all those ridiculous claims the manufacturers of statin drugs made about cholesterol.

Not that it was silent in the bar. Our intense chewing was punctuated with the occasional crack of someone's break, a subdued cheer or groan, faint commentary from the play-by-play of a Giants game on the wide-screen, and the musical accompaniment of some Muzak string orchestra covering sixties songs. I almost gagged on a fry listening to a lush, melodic rendition of "Itsy Bitsy Teeny Weeny Yellow Polka Dot Bikini."

Finally satiated, we both pushed our chairs back from the greasy remains of the day. Levar took a long pull from his Bud, and I sucked up a mouthful of vanilla shake. Now we were ready.

Levar began, "Well the sixties are dead. It looks like the corporate racist fascists won the field, didn't they?"

I wasn't giving up yet. "It ain't over till the fat lady commits suicide. But, no matter how it comes out, at least we didn't roll over and kiss their asses."

He surprised me. "We were stupid. Some of us Panthers were thugs, some of us were community organizers, most of us were a little of both. But we totally underestimated the viciousness of the Man and the complete indifference of whites. They cheered when cops shot us down. Except for you bozos. Like I say, stupid. And we did stupid things. Killing the innocent and letting the guilty kill us. We paid by doing time or bleeding out.

"But autopsies don't help. Hey, I'm glad you lived through it. Let's talk about now. What were you doing in Westlake? Don't lie to me."

We'd been through a lot together. I wasn't about to scam him. So I filled him in. My life on the run as Warren Ritter. Meeting the daughter I never knew I had. About Orrin's murder and how I hadn't had a decent night's sleep in a week. It was weird. Sally and Rose knew all about my past life. But it felt good to tell a guy about it.

"Damn, that's quite a story. So what do you want from me?"

"You knew Orrin, or Oscar to you. What was he like?"

Levar looked away. Then he looked me right in the eyes. "He'd read Eldridge and Bobby and H. Rap Brown. Other stuff too; everything from *A People's History of the U.S.* to *Addicted to War*. He had the rhetoric down cold. And he worked real hard with us. Not doing the instigate-violence crap like those FBI worms used to do. Real sincere. Not a slacker at all. I liked him. He had me totally conned." He took another long gulp. He hadn't met my eyes once through that story. I knew he was lying about something.

"So what are *you* doing with all those peaceniks?"

"Trav— I mean, Warren, I'm a teacher at Evergreen Community College. I drive a Camry. Hell, I'm almost respectable. No one knows about what I did in the Fist of Glory days. Now I *am* one of those peaceniks."

"How's it working out for you?"

"I'm sick of it. I sure don't miss the bad old days, but this life I'm living is about as interesting as oatmeal. I have a buddy, Rico

97

Lopez, down in Cabo San Lucas. He keeps telling me to dump it all and join him running a charter fishing boat. If I had ten grand I'd do it."

I had to get back on point. "I've got to ask about the group. Was there anyone who seemed to have a closer relationship with Orrin— I mean Oscar?"

"Not really. And I'm guessing your next question. Nobody disliked him as far as I could tell. He was a nice, passionate progressive. One of us."

"Not anymore." Damn, there was something this guy was holding back. But I wasn't going to get it out of him today.

Before I left I gave him one of my Tarotman business cards, and he gave me his card. He wrote his cell phone number on the back and said, "Use my voice mail to get in touch with me. This is a clean phone, but please don't use it unless it's a real emergency." I'd passed a real test to get that.

On the drive home I decided to check in with Sally. I was calling on my cell phone and she'd just have to live with it. I pulled into a PetSmart parking lot. I hate people who chat and drive. That's when I discovered that I had the damn cell phone turned off. Seven messages.

The first one was from my partner in crime. "Hey Warren, Sally here. Progress on the Hightower front. For a hundred fifty bucks on the Internet, I bought a list of her phone calls. Anyone can do this job! Lots of calls to three numbers in Brawley. You probably never heard of it. Twenty thousand people living 120 feet below sea level, and twenty-five miles from Mexico. Near 110 degrees in the late summer.

"Anyway, no one calls Brawley for the fun of it. So I'm sending Heather down to poke around. Don't argue, her mind is made up about this, and that's something you're never going to change. Besides, she's already on her way. She has a good photo of Julia that I got from a newspaper article about their wedding. She's going to show it around and we'll see what she can scratch up. Hope your day as a PI is going well."

The second message had me tearing out of that lot and speeding for the freeway.

CHAPTER TWENTY-ONE

M r. Ritter, this is Reverty Wallace at Coastal Memorial Hospital in Santa Cruz. We brought in a woman this morning in critical condition. She left a note with your name and this number to call. Her name is Fran Wilkins. If you could—"

I was hoping a cop would stop me. I needed the escort. No such luck. I had to shove my way through the afternoon Silicon Valley gridlock until I finally hit clear asphalt on Highway 17 going over the hump to Santa Cruz. I didn't know my old Civic could break ninety-five.

"Don't die, Fran. Don't die. I should have known. Don't die, Fran." A simple mantra, but it was all I had.

I left my car in the turnaround in front of the main door. Who cared? I raced down the shiny corridor toward the swinging red doors marked EMERGENCY.

"I'm Warren Ritter. I understand you have my daughter, Fran Wilkins, in here."

The tired black woman behind the Plexiglas barrier began going down the list in front of her. She spoke without looking up. "If you could just take a seat someone will come out in a moment to talk with you."

"Not good enough!"

Good, she finally looked up.

I said to her, "If your daughter was lying in there dying would you just sit down, cross your legs, and wait quietly until some white guy finally found the time to get around to you?"

I saw a trace of a smile.

"I thought not. Now I'm not trying to make your day miserable, but I need to know if my daughter is still alive, and if she is, how bad is she?"

She looked straight at me. Then she looked away, dialed the phone, and spoke softly into her headset. I couldn't hear what she said. She disconnected and looked back at me. "She's alive and stable. But she's still critical. A doctor will be out within five minutes to talk with you. Now, will you sit down?"

I looked at her badge and said, "Ellen, you're very kind. Thank you. I'll be right over here. I owe you one."

"Honey, you don't owe anybody anything. Just sit, and we'll hope for the best."

And that's what I did. It was uncharacteristically quiet for an ER. One Mexican family and me.

The doctor came out in three minutes. He was bearish, with a friendly mouth, white hair, and very tired eyes. He reached out to shake my hand. It was a reassuringly firm grip. Again I did the badge trick. "Hello, Dr. Bertolli, my name is Warren Ritter. I'm Fran Wilkins's—"

"Call me Tom. I know who you are. You made quite an impact on Ellen. Sit down and let's talk about Fran." We sat.

He began, "Do you know what happened?" I shook my head. "Well, evidently Mrs. Wilkins took a bottle of Depakote pills and then drank a pint of Wild Turkey. If her minister hadn't paid an unexpected morning visit I'm afraid we would have lost her. As it is she's stable, but unconscious. I think I may be able to upgrade her condition tonight, but she's not going anywhere for a week or so. It remains to be seen what the long-term effects might be, but I'm hoping we got the bulk of it pumped out in time."

This was every bit as bad as I thought it would be. Then it got worse.

"The police have posted a guard at her door. It's against the law to try to kill yourself, and besides they said they had some other matter that concerned them. Before they confiscated the note that she left, one of our techs jotted down your name and number. I don't know all of what the letter said, but José, that's the med tech, said it had your name and phone number in big letters. And somebody named Rose Jane or something. Do you know who that is?"

"Yes, I will contact her. She's Fran's therapist."

"Good. Well, Fran's out cold right now. But do you want to see her?"

"Please."

He guided me through the maze of the ER. Sitting outside one of the doors was a policeman reading a book. He looked up as we came, but said nothing as we entered. It was clear he was there not to protect Fran, but to make sure she didn't walk away.

The doc let me in and then said, "I've got other work to do. Stay as long as you like."

Fran looked postmortem. She was so still while all the machinery around her blinked, beeped, sighed, and dripped away.

"Don't die, Fran. Don't die." It was the closest I ever got to a prayer.

I heard the door open behind me.

CHAPTER TWENTY-TWO

I have some questions for you when you're done here." It was Officer Vespie, my favorite Santa Cruz policeman.

"Your timing sucks, Vespie."

"Too bad."

I didn't get it. "Look, this isn't a very good time right now. And another thing, you never met me before Monday, yet you have this colossal chip on your shoulder. How come?"

This guy wasn't really into deep introspection. "I don't like your attitude. Besides, all you witchcraft pagans have ruined this town!"

"Witchcraft pagans?"

He took a step toward me. "I was born here. Back then Santa Cruz was a peaceful, fun place to live. Today we bust fourth graders for selling pot, crack is as easy to buy as Pepsi in the high school, and the whole town has gone into a sewer. A man is supposed to protect his family. How the hell am I supposed to raise my son in a cesspool like this? And it all started with you New Age hippies up the hill on campus. Now it's vampire games on Pacific Avenue, and who knows what kind of sex orgies and devil worship in the forest."

"What makes you think I'm a witchcraft pagan?"

"I read the letter." In a singsong voice he said, "'Don't worry, Dad. Just consult your cards and you'll see this is all working out for the best.'"

Great. Thanks, Fran. Well, the best defense is a good offense. "Yeah, I am a psychic. And I see great misfortune about to befall you if you continue to harass innocent citizens."

Vespie went on, "Enough of that crap. Now, I notice Fran's maiden name is Green. Her mother's name is Witkowski. And your name is Ritter."

Long pause. But he hadn't asked me a question. Finally, I said, "So?"

"Can you explain that?"

"Yes." Another long pause. The thin little capillaries in his nose were beginning to get redder.

"Please do."

"No."

"What do you mean no?"

"No, I won't explain that to you."

He had a full flush going now. "There you go again, obstructing justice and interfering in a criminal investigation."

"Why don't you pull me in? I'd love to explain to your chief why I refused to respond to your interrogation while I was standing next to the bed of my daughter who may be dying."

That tan was turning into a truly red complexion now, with those adorable specks of white around the cheekbones. He just stood there panting for a moment, then spun around and stalked out. Round two to me.

CHAPTER TWENTY-THREE

I sat down next to Fran's bed. There wasn't much I could do for her, but I just wanted to be close. I looked up at the sign that said NO CELL PHONES IN THIS AREA. That reminded me, and I pulled out my phone and scrolled down until I found Fran's mother's number.

"Hi, Cathy. This is Richard. I have some bad news." Richard was the name she knew me by.

"Oh no!"

"It's OK, she's still alive. But she's in a hospital. She tried to kill herself."

"Again?"

That didn't sound too good. "How many times has she done this before?"

"Don't ask."

Really not good.

Cathy said, "I was afraid of this when I got her e-mail this morning. I tried to call but there was no answer. How bad is it?"

"Pretty bad. She's still unconscious. If you want to come out here, I'd be willing to help with airfare and such."

"Thank you, Richard, that's very kind of you. But I have my hands full taking care of my mother right now. Plus, and I don't mean to be unkind or anything, but I have spent my share of nights sitting next to a hospital bed waiting for her to come back to life. I guess it's your turn."

This was as feisty as I'd ever heard Cathy. "I'll keep you informed about Fran's condition. We'll talk later."

"That would be good, Richard. I'm glad you're there. Good-bye now."

Since I was already breaking the law about cell phones, I realized I'd better cancel tonight's therapy appointment with Rose. But before I could start, the door began to open. I quickly stashed my phone. It was Reverend Larry Dalton, the L.A. slugger and the guy who saved my daughter's life. By his side was a thoroughbred blonde, only five pounds heavier than an anorexic and with legs that went on forever. She glowed perfection, from her underdone makeup to her ribbon cashmere bolero and milky silk dress. The jarring dissonance, like the flaw in a Navajo rug, was her left arm, about three-quarters the length it should be.

I got up and shook his hand. "Thank you so much, Larry. I don't know how to repay you."

He hugged me. "You'd have done the same, Warren. It's just what we do; we all look out for each other. I'm just thankful that God led me to her doorstep in time to make a difference." Then he turned. "This is my wife, Lorraine. She knows the Wilkins family well."

Damn, if I'd met her a couple of years ago *I'd* have considered the seminary. We shook hands. Her grip was firm, no nonsense. Her other arm just hung limp by her side.

Larry asked, "How are you holding up with all this?"

"It's been a hell of a week."

"Did you know that this," he looked over to Fran, "was going to happen?"

"Not a clue. But I should have. Both Fran and I battle with mood disorders. But I never thought she'd go this far."

"Me neither. I heard from the police that she wrote a note and said that her mother is taking care of Justin. Do you know how I can get in touch with her? I'd like to see if there is anything I can do to help."

Crafty little girl, my daughter. "No, I'm not in touch with Fran's mother these days. I heard she lived back east, but I can't help you. Sorry." I'd go to hell for sure, lying to a man of the cloth.

Lorraine asked, "Is there anything you need?"

"No, I'm OK. Thanks for asking."

Then Larry handed me his card. "My address and phone number are on there. I know you're not a part of my church, but I'd like you to think you can come over any time if you need any help or support. Oh, yes, and I don't know how well you knew Orrin. But I wanted to invite you to his memorial service. We're holding it Friday at six at the church."

"Thank you for inviting me. I didn't know Orrin that well"— understatement of the century—"but it would mean a lot to be there." And maybe see if I can detect the ravages of guilt on the murderer. Isn't that how Agatha would do it?

He went over and said some blessing over Fran. I stood around looking uncomfortable. Lorraine stood around looking like she was waiting for her photo shoot.

She turned to me and said, "I'm so sorry for all this. Fran recently told me about meeting you for the first time. This must be quite a shock, finding your daughter and then having to come here." She gestured with one hand to indicate the hospital room.

"Well, yes, it is a bit abnormal. But I think I know Fran's eccentricity pretty well. Unfortunately her old man is also prone to dramatic gestures."

Lorraine smiled. OK, here was one of Fran's confidantes. It was time to pump her a little. "How well did you know Orrin, her husband?"

The smile died. The oddest look slithered across her face. Then she said, "I'm sorry. I can't talk right now." She turned to her husband and said, "Darling, we need to leave, or we will be late to the Franklins's rehearsal dinner."

They were out of there within sixty seconds. When they left, I glanced at my watch: 5:33. Then I remembered—I was going to be late too. I had babysitting duty that night.

The nurse at the front desk assured me that it was highly unlikely that Fran was coming to consciousness anytime soon. She took my cell number and ordered me to go home and rest.

Rest, right. I hit the streets, heading north to do my granddad thing.

I may hate people who drive and talk on their cell phone at the same time, but I was going to be late for my babysitting chores if I didn't step on it. I called Rose, and got the machine.

"Hey Rose, it's the wanderer. I've got some bad news about your newest client. She's in the ER of Coastal Memorial Hospital in Santa Cruz. She took your meds. Unfortunately she took the whole bottle, with a bourbon chaser. Looks like she's going to live, but she doesn't have a lot to live for. The cops think she killed her old man. And I'm the lucky recipient of their offspring. Lots to talk about, but not tonight. Cancel my appointment. I'll pay double next time. I've got to go change diapers now. Ciao, baby!"

CHAPTER TWENTY-FOUR

I was damn tired of that drive! It didn't help my mood any when Sally met me at the door in her basketball clothes and said, "Warren, I *told* you I had a game tonight. Justin's bottle is in the fridge. Warm it before you give him any. Read the stuff on my desk. See you at ten or so." Dog and girl were gone.

"Well, buddy, it's just you and me."

He held up his giraffe and told me, "*Ga!*"

At first everything went pretty good. I trotted him around slung over my shoulder while I read Orrin's prelim autopsy report. (The bullet hole in his skull was consistent with damage you would expect from a bullet somewhere between .32 and .45 caliber.) I heated up Justin's formula and then I remembered some movie where I saw a mom dripping milk on her wrist from the bottle before giving it to her kid. Ouch! So I put an ice cube in the bottle and that seemed to work. I did the burping thing. I felt like I was getting the hang of this.

That's when he started to cry. I checked his panties. All clean.

I bounced him around. No good. I tried reason. Not today. That incessant crying was beginning to get to me.

Sally was shooting hoops. Heather was just outside of Mexico. And I started to lose it. Who else could help?

"Yes?"

"Hi Tara, it's your brother."

"What's that crying?"

"Um, that's why I'm calling. It's Justin. I'm taking care of him, and I don't know how to make him stop."

"Where's Fran?"

"In the hospital. She tried to kill herself. So do you have any ideas what I could do?"

"This is a lot to download on me all at once, Richard. Where are you?"

"At my girlfriend's house outside Pinole."

"I'm coming over. Just carry him around until I get there."

I gave her the address, praised Jesus for small miracles, and walked the squalling bag of misery all around the house.

Tara took a warm wet cloth and carefully removed whatever was in Justin's right eye. Blessed silence descended. He smiled at her with a glow I hadn't seen before in his face. She cradled Justin in her arms and sang a lullaby in some haunting foreign language. He was asleep in five minutes. She laid him in a crib that had appeared since I left this morning, and then turned to face me. She looked pretty darn serious, yet her eyes and her voice were still soft from being with Justin.

"OK, Richard. What is really going on here?"

I can lie to my sister. The only problem is that I am incapable of successfully lying to her. So I didn't bother trying. I just left out a couple of minor things like the stuff about Dad's bisexuality, his possible murder, and Julia Hightower's mysterious origins. After she heard the tale of Fran's escapades, and my tireless investigations into Orrin's death, she shook her head.

"Richard, you are one of the most eccentric people that I know. But this week, I think Fran was lucky to have you as her dad. Unfortunately, you can't keep Justin. I mean, this is no place for him. Look around. There's you, a man who never held a child until this week, your girlfriend, and a teenager, neither of which know a heck of a lot more than you do."

I got defensive. "Hey, that's not fair. I think we're doing a pretty good job. Besides I'm not giving him back to those in-laws. No way! Fran trusted me with him."

Tara stayed cool. "I've actually met those in-laws. And two more bigoted, righteous, crotchety human beings never walked the face of the earth. No, I'm going to take Justin home with me."

"I don't think so. What do you know about raising kids?"

She actually smiled. "I lived for ten years in Nwanetsi, an African village in Kruger Park, while I studied lion prides. I became a midwife while I was there and three girls in the village are named Tara in my honor. I know about raising children."

She'd trumped me. But I wasn't giving up that easy. "You're working full time."

"I'm on winter break right now, and I can get twelve weeks of Family and Medical Leave whenever I want them. That should take us well into next year, and we can see if Fran is capable of raising this child by then."

I heard the frostiness in her voice.

I tried one more gambit. "I don't know if Fran would like that idea. She was pretty mad at you the last time we spoke."

"Well, Richard, I'll let you decide. Would you trust the judgment of a woman who may be a murderer, who abandoned her child to a man who knows nothing about being a father, and who's lying in a coma after trying to kill herself?"

Hmm, she had me there.

Tara went on, "Look, the only issue is what's best for Justin. Here's my card, with my address on it. I live on the ground floor, so wheelchair access is no problem. I'll let you and Sally and Heather come over and visit him all you want, and even take him for overnights. Hell, I'll need a break from him; every mother does. But Justin knows me, and I can provide the best and safest home for him right now."

I sighed. "Heather's going to kill me. But you're right. Take Justin, but expect Sally and Heather on your doorstep tomorrow."

"I welcome them."

THURSDAY, DECEMBER 22

Dashing through the snow, in a one-horse open sleigh,
Over the fields we go, laughing all the way.
Bells on bob-tails ring, making spirits bright,
What fun it is to ride and sing a sleighing song tonight.

Jingle bells, jingle bells, jingle all the way!
O what fun it is to ride in a one-horse open sleigh.
Jingle bells, jingle bells, jingle all the way!
O what fun it is to ride in a one-horse open sleigh.

—"Jingle Bells,"
James Pierpont (1857)

CHAPTER TWENTY-FIVE

I woke up late, perfectly well rested. I felt on top of the world. Something must have happened in my dreams, because I finally knew exactly what I needed to do.

It was time for me to move on. I'd solved the case. I knew that my daughter had killed her husband, and I didn't blame her. Thank goodness Justin had a good home with Tara. Sally—no—I wasn't going to think about Sally. That would just bum me out. She'd probably be relieved to have me out of her hair. I'm not a very easy man to love. Kind of like my dad.

Everything was going to work out just fine for everybody without me around to screw things up. Besides, I was really tired of taking care of everybody else: Fran, Sally, Heather, now Justin. I didn't want to spend the rest of my life boxed in like that. I needed some breathing space. It was break time! Maybe a tour up to Alaska, just to clean me out a little.

I drove down to Al's. I didn't say much, just got on my bike and headed north along the Pacific. It was a grand day for my escape, the sky clear blue all the way up to the Gates of Paradise. On my left the ocean was waving me on with tiny whitecap hands. I sang "Travelin' Man" at the top of my lungs and savored the wind, the bike, the curves of Route 1, and a gull soaring next to me, trying to keep pace. Just leave all the crap behind, and ride into unlimited possibility. God, the nectar of freedom was sweet!

I was still savoring my aliveness when I got hungry for something more substantial than salty sea air. I was outside a tiny burg called Gualala. I pulled into a little shopping center that had a sign reading ESPRESSO. Soon, I was looking out a big bay window of Café La La watching the ocean stretch on forever. I was enjoying a triple latte, a damn good grilled turkey sandwich, and the best broccoli salad I'd ever eaten. Then I noticed them.

He was an older guy, my age probably: tall, a little overweight, gray hair, and ocean-colored eyes. She had dark red hair with blond streaks, a cute face, and a smile that reminded me of Sally's. But what got to me was how they touched each other's faces, and laughed. They so obviously relished each other's company.

All of a sudden my wall of pleasure and satisfaction started to crumble. Tears for something I couldn't even name started running down my cheeks. It was like I just woke up from being in a blackout.

Sally! What was I doing? What happened to me? Who possessed me to drive my bike up here? I almost didn't know how I got two and a half hours north of the city. My God, I'd nearly driven away from everything I loved. Was I finally going psychotic? I got really, really scared.

Thankfully, I'd brought my cell phone. I called Rose and (whew) actually got her.

"Rose, I think I'm really crazy this time. This morning I just got on my bike and headed for Alaska. I just now realized how insane that was. I need to see you!"

"That's a big ten-four, Warren. You do need to see me. Where are you?"

"A little place called Gualala. About halfway to nowhere along the coast. Maybe three hours away."

"I have a free hour at four. Come down right away. Are you OK to drive?"

"Yeah sure, I guess. And thanks!"

I called the waitress over and handed her a hundred-dollar bill. "Take twenty. The rest is for the couple over there, too. Don't say anything right now, but after I leave just give it to them and tell them that I said, 'Thank you for loving each other so much.' "

CHAPTER TWENTY-SIX

No, this was not a manic episode, although I think your bipolar condition may have played a factor in it. It's not in the DSM yet, but those of us who work with it call it Adult Runaway Syndrome with Dissociative Features. I think you've suffered from a chronic version of this condition most of your adult life. You just experienced an acute, and luckily short-lived, eruption today."

It was calming just to sit in the big leather chair, listen to Rose's level voice, and look out over the bay as the sun played tag with a few clouds. Under the Golden Gate Bridge I could see one sailboat, spinnaker aloft, straining hard against the outgoing tide to make it across the strait.

"You've been under a phenomenal amount of stress this week. What happened was an outbreak of defensive denial. Unable to cope anymore, and unwilling to face the immensity of your situation, you just shoved everything into your unconscious and took a primitive course of action to escape all those issues. And perhaps there was a smidgen of passive-aggressive anger tossed in, just leaving the mess behind for the rest of us to deal with."

I guess she did understand. But it still scared me. "Rose, it was so compelling. It seemed like the obvious thing to do. I wasn't aware of being angry, or resentful or anything. It felt good. I must be really fringe to do this."

"Warren, you're not that special. Two million people disappear every year in this country. They run from the law, child support payments, or from some other experiences where they feel an acute sense of powerlessness and failure. Some of this is simple sociopathy or irresponsibility. But a lot of times it begins with an experience just like you had. Once the running begins there is an intense upwelling of relief. Denial can feel very delicious, even addictive, as you found out. You, however, broke through that defense rather quickly, and saw it for what it was; a hopelessly ineffective strategy for dealing with the problems that you face."

"What's the dissociative part mean?"

"In a classical dissociative amnesia fugue (which is very rare) you completely forget who you are and go wandering off. When you finally 'wake up' you can't remember how you got there. Your experience today had aspects of that, but was more like identity confusion. You maintained most of your consciousness. It was only one segment of your identity, your deep need for intimacy, that got walled off for a time. For a while, you acted as though that need did not exist."

"Yeah, but I might not have woken up. I could be in Oregon right now."

"You're sitting here, aren't you?"

The sailboat had made it out of the current and was rapidly heading for its berth in the San Francisco Marina.

Rose was relentless. "Now let's talk about those problems that you've decided to face."

Oh, hell, I was going to have to tell her about my gay dad.

CHAPTER TWENTY-SEVEN

I walked back into my apartment a humbler man. As I re-wound some endless message on my answering machine I thought about who we take ourselves to be. Most of us imagine that we are stable, consistent, more or less the same person from day to day. We hardly notice when some virus has taken over the software of our personality. If I feel this way and if I think this way, then my thoughts, my feelings, and all the plans and decisions that come spinning out of them are right. I know who I am, after all. It couldn't be that I'm a nutcase!

Virus-eaten beliefs might be, "I've had enough. I'm going to walk right in there and give my boss a piece of my mind!" or "He never loved me. I'm throwing this ring in his face!" or "Hey, today's a good day for a road trip to Alaska!" We accept those thoughts and feelings as reasonable and sensible, never even notic-ing that we just wandered off the deep end.

I was luckier than most. I knew I was crazy. It made it easier to acknowledge that I might have let sanity slip away for a little while. I felt sorry for the poor people who were under the illusion that they're sane. They're not going to have any fallback position when reality exposes their irrationality. They'll blame, they'll attack, all the while desperately fighting the inner knowledge that they've been acting like a wacko, nutcase, crackpot. Which makes them look even crazier. Poor, sane sitting ducks.

The message on my machine was from a very excited Heather.

"Get out of the way, Stephanie Plum, I'm coming through! Being a detective rocks, Warren. It's totally sick. Oh, that means 'cool but unbelievable' just in case I need to translate, you aging hippie. Anyway, who would think I'm such a natural? I am woman, hear me roar!

"So, to get a little focus here, Ace Detective Heather Talbridge reporting in. I blew into Brawley. Wow, hard to describe this place. It's laid out with a ruler on a flat dry griddle. Kind of cowboy-mariachi meets Wal-Mart. It would be high on the list of the top ten places I never want to see again. And today the temperature's almost eighty. This place must be like Dante's Inferno in summer. Hey Warren, you like that classical reference, there? I found the coolest version of that book the other day. Great modern illustrations of all the inner circles of hell, with industrial waste, gang bangers, and scenes from the urban hell we call home. Very *noir fantastique*. Check it out.

"Oh yeah, back on topic. So I started showing Julia Hightower's picture around. Just got a lot of bad pick-up lines from scudzy cowboys. Most of the town is Spanish-speaking, so already I had a couple of strikes against me, being a unilingual chick. I started thinking Sally should have sent a real PI to do this job.

"Then for some reason I started looking in Laundromats. No lecherous guys, and women with nothing to do but watch clothes spin. Jackpot! I met Vicky Tripple. She looked like a dried-applehead lady. The sun must be killer out here. But she was very sweet. Back in the eighties she went to school with the gal in the picture, Janie Higgins (not Julia Hightower!). Janie was the daughter of Dr. Allen Higgins, a local doctor.

"Cool. Now to track him down. Checked at the hospital. No recent record of Dr. Higgins, but I was so desperate to get in touch with Uncle Al that they finally tracked the name down. A cardiologist, he left town back in 1986.

"I called Sally and she fused. Bet you'll never guess who your dad's cardiologist was. You got it!

"Then I hit the microfiche machine at the library. Scanning through rolls of the *Imperial Valley News,* I felt just like a real PI. I love this stuff! Anyway, I got carpal tunnel syndrome and one gem. Obituary announcement in January of 1985. Mrs. Veronica Higgins, beloved wife of Dr. Allen Higgins and mother of Jane Elizabeth Higgins, died of a heart attack. A lot of heart attacks around that guy, aren't there?

"I rock. I need to . . ." A long beep finally cut her off. There was no call back, so I guess I had her whole report. My father was murdered.

FRIDAY, DECEMBER 23

The holly bears a berry,
As red as any blood,
And Mary bore sweet Jesus Christ,
To do poor sinners good.

The holly bears a prickle,
As sharp as any thorn,
And Mary bore sweet Jesus Christ,
On Christmas Day in the morn.

The holly bears a bark,
As bitter as the gall,
And Mary bore sweet Jesus Christ,
For to redeem us all.

—"The Holly and the Ivy,"
traditional Christmas carol

CHAPTER TWENTY-EIGHT

What a pleasant way to end a sleepless night: a triple latte, a second-rate croissant, wracking guilt, rage, and the *San Francisco Chronicle*. I still hadn't called Sally. She was mad enough at me when she found out I gave Justin to Tara. Besides, if I called, I knew I'd end up telling her the truth. "Where was I yesterday? Oh, I headed for Alaska." That's all she needed right now, confirmation that she's going out with a compulsive runner. Besides, I really wasn't ready to talk about what Heather had unearthed. I didn't want to think about anything but caffeine and News of the World.

I'd bought the paper because I saw the words "Santa Cruz" on the front page. It was an article about finding the shark-eaten body of a Japanese man washed up on the beach. But it was the second article about Santa Cruz, on page two, that made me want to throw up.

SUICIDE-HOMICIDE

Police have charged Fran Wilkins with the murder of her husband, Officer Orrin Wilkins, of the Santa Cruz Police Force. Mrs.
Wilkins allegedly attempted suicide yesterday, and is currently under police guard at Coastal Memorial Hospital. Police Chief Heidi
Mallon issued this statement: "The presumed murder weapon was
found in the possession of Mrs. Wilkins. We expect a complete
ballistics report this morning, but we have issued a warrant, and
will take her into custody pending her medical release."

The whereabouts of their five-month-old child is in question. Officer Wilkins's parents, Frank and Eva Wilkins, told this
reporter . . .

I tossed the paper on the table. Damn! Fran's going to jail
while my father's murderer was scot-free. I felt like someone out
of *Hamlet*. Maybe Alaska wasn't such a bad idea. Just kidding.

I was going to have to face the music sooner or later. I headed
over to Sally's. Now I really needed her.

"Where were you yesterday?"

Sally was typing like mad on her keyboard and intently looking
at the monitor. She didn't notice me look away.

"I took a ride on my Alpina. I guess I just needed to let off
some steam."

"I can understand that. You've been under a lot of stress. Just call
next time and let me know what you're doing. That way I won't
worry."

"Will do." If I'm sane enough to remember.

She looked up at me and smiled. "Are you OK?"

"As OK as the father of a suspected murderer and the son of a murder victim can be." I gave her a brief rundown of Heather's findings. Then I tossed the article over to her. "It's on page two, upper right."

She whistled.

I asked her, "What does 'in her possession' mean? She's in the hospital."

"They probably found the gun in her car or her house. Let me see what I can find out." She retreated into virtual reality while I absentmindedly scratched Ripley behind her ears. Finally Ripley moved away. Bad vibes, I guess. Then I just sat there, wishing I was back in last week and none of this stuff had happened.

Sally reemerged. "Well, good news and bad, which first?"

"Bad." Always my preferred choice. Tell me about the terminal diagnosis before you let me know I won the lottery.

"It's a cop murder, so they set up an anonymous hotline. A male voice phoned in a tip yesterday. He told them that he saw Fran open the compartment behind her convertible top and throw something in it that looked like a gun. It was easy to get a warrant, and sure enough, there was a Glock .40 caliber pistol, the firearm issued by the Santa Cruz Police Department. Maybe his own gun?"

Cop killed with his own piece. "So any more misery, or can we jump to the good news now?"

"Fran is no longer in critical condition. She's conscious and they've upgraded her to guarded."

"Great, soon she'll be healthy enough to go to prison."

"Warren, would you rather she be worse?"

I got up. Sally was right, I was being rather grinchy. "Sorry. Look, I've got to do something to help while she's still in the hospital. I don't want her going to jail."

"What are you going to do?"

I didn't know. I started pacing and thinking aloud. "OK. Let's just assume that Fran didn't do it. Where do we stand? The cops think she did, so we know Vespie and his crew will only collect evidence that will help the DA build a case against her. We've got to get some evidence so compelling that they back off.

"One, we need to canvass Fran's neighborhood and find out who really put that gun in Fran's car.

"Two, our nice rageaholic minister. Maybe he blew up at Orrin and accidentally shot him in the head. It's weak, I know. But we need to talk to some of Reverend Dalton's parishioners.

"Three, maybe it was a peacenik. I know Levar is capable of murder. Back in the sixties he told me about a white guy he shot. I know he was lying about something to me at the pool hall. Maybe there's more in the Orrin/Levar relationship that we don't know about.

"Four, we can pull an O.J. and blame the cops. Orrin was Vespie's partner. Maybe he found out too much. So Vespie killed him. I'll talk with Mac and see if we can find out what's in the file Internal Affairs has on Vespie."

Sally had typed while I'd cogitated. The printer started spurting out paper.

"Those are the neighbors around Fran's. You can start there. I'll pull up a list of folks in Dalton's church and send Heather off to see what she can find out on that end. I'll go after the Levar angle."

It felt really good. I wasn't alone. "Sally, you keep this up and I might really fall for you."

"You're just after my keyboard. You guys are all alike. What do you want to do about the Julia Hightower-Higgins thing?"

"Look, Sally, I am beyond overwhelmed right now. Let's just table that murder for a while until we get this one under control."

"Sounds good to me."

I called Mac from Sally's.

"Epic Thrash, blast pedal headquarters."

"It sounds just like you're speaking English."

"Hi, Warren, hey, perfect timing. I'm just heading out to Santa Cruz. If it doesn't rain, my buddy Sam and I are going to do some slick rock up in Big Basin. It's my last big blowout. Sunday, I have to go on patrol duty, in a frigging squad car. Can you believe that! I don't know how much longer I can stand to work at that job. Anyway, I'll call you tonight and tell you what I find out about Vespie and Wilkins."

"Break a leg."

"What?!"

"Never mind. Thanks a lot, Mac."

Now guess what? I had to swing past my house to print off some bogus business cards, grab my "flight bag" with a wig, glasses, and makeup in it, and then it was time for my favorite activity: a drive down to Santa Cruz.

CHAPTER TWENTY-NINE

I don't want to talk with you." Fran turned away from me and faced the wall.

"Luckily, you don't have to. But unless you put your pillow over your head you will have to listen to me. I'll make it easy. I'll say three things. Then if you still don't want to talk I'll leave. So here goes . . ."

How do I get myself into these things? I had no idea what I was going to say.

"One, Justin is fine. He's doing great. He's also well hidden, so don't worry on that score." No response. Strike.

"Two, we've got a whole crew working on your case." No movement. Strike two.

Three strikes and I'm out. "And finally, I tried to kill myself four times, not to count when I took incredibly stupid risks, which shouldn't count anyway. How many times for you?' "

"Seven." Home run!

"That's pretty good, seeing as how you're so much younger

than me. What was your favorite? Mine was walking into a blizzard. You stop feeling cold and get kind of warm after a while."

She turned around and just looked at me, maybe checking to see if I was telling the truth. Since I was, she spoke. "Mine was driving my motor scooter off a cliff. It was a hell of a ride down!" She smiled.

"Sounds like a lot more fun than Depakote."

"Acres more fun! You know, Dad, I didn't want to see you."

"I know. I always felt guilty as hell after one of my suicides. Didn't want to see anybody. Ashamed. But even worse, I usually felt very pissed when I woke up. Alive, still? Damn! What a waste of all that effort."

"God, you have been there, haven't you."

I nodded.

"So what am I supposed to do now?"

"Don't say anything to the cops, to the nurses, or to the doctors about what you did or why. If anyone asks you anything other than, 'And how are we today?' tell them you have to talk with your lawyer. Remember it's against the law to try to kill yourself and fail."

"But I don't have a lawyer."

"You do now. His name is Clyde Berkowitz. He's a shark; you'll like him. I'll get him down here as fast as I can."

We were doing pretty good, finally. Now I had to grill her. I needed to find out some more about Orrin, and the day of the murder. "Fran, what can you tell me about Orrin?"

"I don't want to talk about it."

Damn, back to the dugout. "Look, Fran, just give me something to go on."

She sat up, vitriol in her eyes. "You want something to go on. I'll tell you a story of what happened last week. And I know every detail because Orrin relished telling me exactly what he said and did.

"I needed to get out of the house. He said, 'Don't worry, Fran, I can take care of Justin fine. You go out and take care of yourself, or whatever you call it. Be sure and call me if you need a ride. This family can't afford you getting another DWI.' He took every opportunity to stick in another barb.

"I slammed the door on the way out. Then Orrin picked Justin up and set him on his lap. Justin giggled and clutched his favorite toy, a plush furry giraffe.

"Orrin started gently rocking the leg Justin sat on up and down, making him laugh. 'It's "trot trot" time for Justin. We're galloping over the plain. That's a very nice giraffe you've got there.'

"Justin held it towards him and said, *'Ga.'*

"That must have pissed him off for some reason. I know exactly what happened after that. He repeated it to me several times, exactly what he said, and what he did to Justin. He sat Justin down on the coffee table in front of him and said, 'What's up with this *"Ga"* noise, boy? This friggin' toy never put one meal on your table or paid one dime for the roof over your head. I swear your first word was *"Ga."* You didn't say *"da da"* or *"ma ma."* Although with your mother, I don't blame you. I never had a mother who deserted me in the middle of Macy's and went wandering off. So not saying *"ma ma"* was a pretty wise judgment. But it was a mistake for you to learn the name for your little giraffe, instead of your father. I think it's time you learned a few different priorities in your life, don't you?'

"Then he brought out that damn bike story, the same one he'd tell me to justify his cruelty. He said, 'I'll tell you a little story about my daddy. OK? When I was twelve years older than you are right

141

now, I had a beautiful bike. I'd worked weekends and evenings at my daddy's store to earn the money for my BMX Sting Ray. I could pop wheelies almost half a block long. At dusk I'd take my dog Rex and hop on my bike and we'd cruise the neighborhood. Those were some of my happiest moments. I loved that bike.

"'One day I got mad at my dad. I didn't like the way he was treating my mom. I yelled at him, and told him I was quitting my job at his store. He grabbed me and hauled me into his pickup. He walked away for a moment, and then came back and got in the driver's seat. He put the truck in reverse and I could hear it crush something. We pulled out so that the bent frame and smashed wheels of my bike were right in front of the truck, where I could see them. Then he said, "The next time you talk back to me, I'll put Rex behind this truck. You understand?" My dad didn't like doing that to me. But he knew I had to be tough to survive in this world.'

"Then Orrin picked Justin up and slung him over his shoulder. He walked into the kitchen, stuck the kitchen shears in his pocket, and picked up the trash can. Back in the living room he set Justin on the couch next to him. Then he took Justin's giraffe. Then piece by piece Orrin began cutting the giraffe up and depositing the fur and the polyester filling into the garbage can.

"While he was hacking the toy up he said, 'It's never too early to learn not to get attached to objects. The only thing you can really trust is me. Mommy is crazy. She'll spoil you rotten and leave you completely unprepared to handle the real world. Everyone else is just out to fulfill their own greedy desires, usually at your expense. Respect your father. I'm the only one who really cares about you. Now it's time for you to go down for a nap.' That's the kind of royal bastard my ex-husband was. He deserved to die."

She rolled over facing the wall. I was dismissed.

"I'm sorry, Fran." I headed for the door. I almost didn't hear her when she asked, "Can you bring me my laptop?"

"I'll need your house keys."

"Under the yellow pot on the left-hand side by the back door."

I wondered if the house was sealed off by the police. After all, it's against the law to break that seal. "Will do. I'll bring it tonight."

CHAPTER THIRTY

I went to the men's room to put on my blond wig, adjust my skin color, and put on my glasses. It wouldn't do for the neighbors to recognize me as that freak who drove up on his fancy motorcycle earlier that week.

A bright yellow ribbon sealed off the front door. I walked around to the back as though I was a regular guest. I added Fran's key to my keychain, broke the tape (trying not to leave any prints), and walked in.

I just strolled around, soaking up her home. It was decked for the season, with a hand-carved nativity scene laid out on the mantel, a big stocking marked JUSTIN hanging empty over the hearth, and a small tree loaded with tiny clear glass ornaments of dolphins, stars, icicles, and reindeer. Her hardwood floors gleamed. Her counters glistened even on this gray day. She'd cleaned furiously to escape her demons. When there was nothing left to clean, she took the pills.

Her laptop was on the desk in her bedroom. I unplugged it and put it in a paper sack. I dumped in some random clothes to hide it.

I didn't know if the hospital regulations about cellular phones extended to wireless, but I didn't want to find out. Fran's problem.

I shut the back door and repaired the crime scene tape with some clear packing tape I'd found in the kitchen. After stashing the shopping bag in my car, I got ready to canvass her neighborhood.

You know how in the mysteries, the hard-boiled private eye knocks on a couple doors and then finds the garrulous spinster who spends her day looking out her window? Real life is so different.

Fifteen doors slammed in my face to the accompaniment of, "No thanks, we don't want any." The weather was getting colder by the door. I didn't even get to pitch my great lie about being a local news reporter. Too many Seventh Day Adventists and real estate salesmen must work this block. If I were a little more thin-skinned, I might take this personally.

Door number sixteen. A big, gray-haired, overweight guy looked at me out of bleary, shadowed eyes. I didn't even get to start before he said, "I don't care what you're selling . . ."

I braced for rejection number sixteen, when he said, "Please, come in and rescue me from the Wetware Plagues of 2525. I'm Richard Phillips. Do you want a cup of coffee?"

I'll never refuse a cup of coffee. He settled me in his living room/office. A pizza box on the floor. A poster of Buffy the Vampire Slayer on the wall. This guy is single. He went into the back of the house and I got up and wandered over to look at his computer monitor.

Altor's virtual avatar hovered over the data shell that surrounded the General Services web core. The defensive ice was thick, but if he could get past the phaser-bots he thought he could penetrate the nucleus and find the file he needed. He knew staying there too long could mean his death, or something worse.

From the kitchen the guy said, "I write science fiction. Or I'm trying to write. I've been staring at that screen for three days. You just interrupted a one-hour Tetris marathon. I need to talk to a real human being."

A schizoid geek; I liked him immediately. Even if the coffee was reheated. And the writing was pretty bad. Maybe he should stick to Tetris.

I figured the reporter story wouldn't work so well with this guy, so I defaulted to telling the truth. "Do you know the gal who had a baby about a half a year ago? She lives four houses down on the other side of the street."

"Oh yeah, sure. The white house with the hedge along one side. You know, there's the weirdest flower that grows out of that hedge: one long purple petal, and a black tongue full of acid."

"Sounds like an alien to me."

"That's what I thought. It would make a good character in one of my books. Right out of the Little Shop of Horrors. Anyway, what about the lady that lives there?"

"She's my daughter. Someone killed her husband, and the police think she did it. I'm trying to help her."

"Wow, I'm sorry. So that was your grandkid?"

"Yes, a five-month-old boy. Can you tell me anything you remember about them?"

"I'm not very good at that stuff. Hey, if you want to know about virtual reality, cyber punk, or information database technology I'm your man. But neighbors, I don't really pay that much attention."

I just pretended that I didn't hear that. "Her name is Fran. Her husband is . . . was Orrin, and their baby's named Justin. Orrin was a police officer. Did you ever see anything unusual going on over there, really, anything at all?"

"Like I said, I don't know. Well, let me think. One time a while ago they got in a big fight, I remember. Yelling at each other. The guy took off in his cop car, really pissed. I remember 'cause I was walking past, and I looked at their kid. They were going at each other, and the kid, I mean a real little baby, he just watched them. Didn't cry or anything. It was kind of spooky, like he was older than they were."

"How long ago was this?"

"I don't know. It was before I started *The Virtual Plague,* so that would be, maybe, three weeks ago. You want some more coffee?"

I didn't, and you've got to know the java must be pretty bad for me to turn free coffee down. "Anything else you remember?"

"Well, this is a bit weird. But I was wondering about if they were fighting because she was having an affair. Hey, I'm sorry, I forgot. She's your daughter."

"No, that's all right. I know Fran is a bit eccentric. No problem. Tell me what made you think she was having an affair."

"Well, I noticed a car over at her house a lot during the day. It was never there at night. Once I saw the guy driving it."

Long pause. OK, prying time! "What kind of car?"

"Some foreign car. A blue four-door."

"And the guy, what did he look like?"

"One tall, scrawny drink of water. Never saw him before or since."

Was our good reverend double-dipping? I tried a couple more questions, but this barrel was bone dry. I thanked Richard and headed back into the town without pity. I didn't get very far.

CHAPTER THIRTY-ONE

Rudolph the Red-Nosed Vespie pulled up in his white sleigh. He was out of the door in a flash. "That's the worst damn wig I've ever seen. Warren Ritter, isn't it? Do you know that you missed Halloween? It was a couple of months ago."

So much for my title of Master of Disguise. "Officer Vespie, what a pleasant surprise!"

"What are you trying to pull?"

"I'm taking a stroll around this lovely neighborhood. Is that against the law, sir?"

"It is when a neighbor calls in a disturbing-the-peace complaint on you. And it sure is, when I see you dressed up for Halloween. Turn around and put your hands on the car."

Unfortunately, I knew enough about the law to know that my negotiating position was piss-poor. Any cop, any time, can drag your sorry ass down to jail. He may not be able to keep you there for long. Unless you are a threat to national security, in which case, 'bye 'bye, Charlie. I gave resistance a shot. "Am I being formally charged?"

He wasn't buying it. "I'll only ask you one more time, turn around, bend over, and put your hands on the car."

I did. He patted me down, and then took my hands and cuffed them. Very tightly. Then he opened the back of the cruiser and shoved me in. I lost my fake glasses in the process. It's damn hard to keep from landing on your face on the floor when your hands are cuffed behind your back.

He got in and drove. He said nothing. We weren't heading downtown, a very bad sign. He drove alongside the back of the Boardwalk. At the end of the road we were overlooking the San Lorenzo River. The day had turned from crummy to dismal.

Finally Vespie spoke, looking out at the gray water. "That's where they pulled Orrin's body out. Under the trestle. He was a damn good cop. Saved my life once, when a carjacking turned violent. I named my son Orrin. He stood by me through my divorce, and I was by his side when Justin was born." Then he muttered something bitter that I couldn't hear.

He turned and looked at me. "He had his work cut out for him, trying to raise that kid. Your daughter is a real case. A wacko, if you ask me."

"Is that a clinical term, Dr. Vespie?"

"Great sense of humor. You comfortable back there?"

"Oh, yeah. All I need is a wet bar."

Vespie stopped looking at the riverbank and turned around. He just looked hard at me. Oh my, was I ever intimidated! Then he said, "Orrin never mentioned you. Said Fran's dad was killed in an explosion before she was born. I checked the marriage license. Her maiden name is Green. You show up to give me grief on Orrin's doorstep. Then you parade around the neighborhood with that phony wig. Who the hell are you?"

"I think you're supposed to say, "You have the right to remain silent. Anything you say can and will be used . . .""

"Shut up! You're super cute, ain't you? She called you her father. Explain that to me."

A cop can cuff you, toss you in jail, even beat the holy bejesus out of you, and all that is legal. The only thing he can't do is make you answer a question. "I am not answering any more questions. I want my lawyer present. I request that you let me contact my lawyer, Clyde Berkowitz."

"If you don't get out of my town, punk, I'm going to run every kind of screening I can until I find out that you have a parking ticket in Burbank, or you forgot to return a library book in Oxnard, or you jaywalked in Eureka. And then I'm going to nail your miserable . . ."

Just then his radio squawked. "We have a two-eleven in progress at Soquel and Seabright, Code Two."

Vespie grabbed the mike. "Unit twelve responding, Code two affirmative." Then he turned back to me. "Your lucky day, blondie." He got out of the car and roughly hauled me out. He ripped the wig off of me, tossed it on the road, and said, "Fucking palau." Then he shoved me on top of the trunk of the car and unlocked the cuffs.

He got back in the car and rolled down the window. "I never want to see you again." Then he took off, making sure he drove right over my blond natural-hair rug.

This was my lucky day, right! My daughter was going to jail. I had no idea who killed her husband. I still wasn't positive that she wasn't guilty. And a cop just called me a pervert. Very lucky. Then it started to rain. I'd have to concede round three to Vespie.

CHAPTER THIRTY-TWO

T he rain poured down on me all along the Boardwalk. It didn't let up as I climbed the hill to the top
of the bluff. It escorted me halfway along West
Cliff Drive, a street with Victorians on one side and,
usually, a breathtaking view of Santa Cruz Bay on
the other. Then the rain stopped dead, and the sun vainly attempted
to break through the grumbling clouds.

I was near the lighthouse, now converted into a surfing museum.
For a moment I just looked out over this famous surfing spot. It was
calming to watch the waves breaking in perfect regularity along
Steamer Lane. As I turned back to the road that led toward my car,
I noticed a kid drop out of a tree in the park to my right.

I'm an inveterate tree climber. I trace it back to my early childhood. One of my first memories is of climbing up a tree with my
sister and finding a lunch all ready for us in the tree house. To me,
at age five, it was magical.

Much of my childhood was spent forty feet off the ground.
Trees were the perfect place to hide out, to set up secret meetings,

to plan escapades around the neighborhood, or to just disappear. I had public trees that everybody in my gang knew about. And I had private trees that I shared only with a very special friend. And one really great tree was for me alone.

That kid had been up in a tree in a rainstorm. This had to be one of those really great trees. I figured what the hell, I couldn't get any wetter. So I went to check it out. It may sound unrealistically juvenile for a man in his fifties to drop everything and climb a wet tree. Scientists now believe that domesticated dogs are simply wolves who evolved in such a way that they never leave their adolescence. I'm kind of like that. That's why I could ride all over the country on my motorcycle for thirty years. You might think it's irresponsible—but all those immature domesticated dogs get their food handed to them by humans, while the wolves have to fend for themselves. There's a lot to be said for permanent adolescence.

The tree looked pretty unpromising at first. A tall Monterey cypress, thick with branches that had to be squeezed around. But I noticed that many of the branches had smooth patches close to the trunk. A positive sign; this must be a popular climb. I twisted around the thick stuff and had to jump up to catch a branch and pull myself up in one thinned-out place. It was a good technical climb.

Near the top it looked like the entire route was blocked by branches. But I saw a crack of gray sky, so I pushed through. I came out on a natural platform, open to the sky, just as the sun hit the high perch where I sat. It felt like revelation morning. This was a great spot. Probably a famous dope-smoking hideaway among Santa Cruz High dropouts.

Drying out wasn't in the cards today. But I could catch the occasional patches of sun that made it through the cloud cover. It was a great nest to perch in and think, undisturbed. Maybe from here I could figure this whole debacle out.

Unfortunately the prime suspect was still my daughter. She had motive, opportunity, and means. She was plenty strong enough to manhandle her husband's skinny little deceased ass into a trunk of a car, and then drag it into the river. This line of thought was not helpful. I needed a new attitude, here.

OK, what about Vespie the Unconscionable? He had means. I didn't know about motive. Maybe he was mad at Orrin, but I just couldn't see him pulling off an acting job like that. He was upset about Orrin's death, no question about it. Damn, I wanted it to be him!

Then there was Reverend Friendly. The only reason he was on the list is that I don't know that many people in Santa Cruz. And he had a juicy violent secret.

Oh, no, now I had it. It was the beautiful Lorraine, the good reverend's wife. She wrestled Orrin's gun from him, shot him, tossed him in her trunk, and then levitated him into the river, all with one arm. A regular Lara Croft!

Or, maybe it was Dr. Tom Bertolli, Fran's physician at the emergency ward. He was as good as anyone else. I was holding a busted hand.

The one suspect I didn't want on the list was Levar. We went way back. Unfortunately, I knew too much about him. There was that time in Chicago, December of sixty-nine, right after the cops executed two Black Panthers. He went berserk. Then he disappeared for two weeks. When he resurfaced I think I was the only person he told the truth to. He'd been a part of a team who executed a brother of one of the cops who shot Mark and Fred. He felt sick about it, and he was haunted by nightmares. But he did it. This man was capable of murder, no doubt about it.

So where did that leave me? Up a tree, that's where. I realized that brilliant cognition was not going to solve this conundrum. I was just going to have to go out and make a mess.

I felt better. Knowing that I couldn't figure this out actually helped my peace of mind. No one was going to use the little gray cells to find this murderer. It was going to take dumb luck, dogged determination, and foolhardy courage. Now that sounded right up my alley.

CHAPTER THIRTY-THREE

I got to the memorial service for Orrin Wilkins late, wet, sweaty, and very grumpy. It had been a long, soggy, uphill climb to my car. Then I'd had to go to the hospital. Fran had been so depressed she hadn't even thanked me for dropping off her computer. She did a couple of interesting things, however. When I asked her if she had talked to anyone about my profession, she gave a cruel little laugh and said, "I wouldn't tell anyone that I was the daughter of a street vendor. I told Orrin once, and he never let me forget it." Then she turned away. Addressing the back of her head, I asked, "Fran, is there anything else you can tell me about Orrin that might help me find out who killed him?"

I could barely hear her. She said, "He raped me. Now go away." End of that conversation.

As I drove to the memorial service I could feel how my wrists still hurt from those handcuffs. I wasn't dressed well enough for this ceremony, and besides, my clothes were steamy. And I didn't even know why I was going there. Did I think the real murderer was going to throw himself over the coffin and pray for forgiveness?

Just my luck, Dalton was a minister in the Church of Salvation in Christ. I had recently run afoul of another minister from that denomination, a female descendant of Rasputin. The building that housed this church was one of those gray monoliths built in the forties that looked like a cross between a cathedral and a bunker. Inside were oak pews, a huge stained-glass Jesus looking down on his (male) disciples, and a free-standing wooden cross hung suspended from the ceiling. The pulpit, however, was cool-looking, carved out of a huge redwood burl. Everything else made me feel oppressed.

I was never a big one for organized religion anyway. Our folks used to send Tara and me to Sunday school every week like clockwork. We had to walk there, sing "Jesus Loves Me," and then walk home. The whole thing seemed pretty silly to me.

My folks never went to church. With the kids out of the house, I think their Sunday services were more of the Tantric variety. After Dad left, Mom would drag us to First Presbyterian, another gray monolith, which this mausoleum reminded me of.

Today, Orrin got a big crowd. Lots of cops in uniform, which didn't help my claustrophobia any. I guess he was a pretty popular guy. I spotted Vespie in the front row, sitting next to two fossils that I guessed might be Orrin's parents.

Reverend Dalton was in full stride. "Orrin now rests in the arms of our creator, where he waits for us to join him. And that day is not far off. We are soon to know what Orrin already knows with every atom of his being, that God is good, that the holy shall be anointed, and that Jesus is soon to rise again and take his brethren home."

I was standing in the door, looking around, severely debating whether to enter or not. Lorraine was up there, sitting next to her husband, looking pretty messy. I'd recently met a woman who looked more beautiful when she cried. Not so with the reverend's missus: eyes red, face pale, nose running. She wasn't alone. There were plenty of sniffles welling up in the crowd.

Then I saw someone who didn't fit.

When I lived in Alaska, I'd roomed with a family that had a little girl who was permanently affixed to the television. I remember how annoying those Sesame Street shows were, but one of those jingles came into my mind as I stood there: "One of these things is not like the others. One of these things is not the same!" The thing that was not the same in this picture was a black revolutionary once named Levar, and then Lebna, and now passing as Lawrence West.

I guess he could have gotten the announcement of the service out of the newspaper. But what the hell was he doing here? Except for a sprinkling of black officers, this was an all-white crowd. Showing up here fits into the unnecessary risk category. The last thing I was going to do was to indicate any relationship with him. I was a pariah. He didn't need me drawing attention to him. I tuned back in to the sermon.

"Matthew reminds us, 'Therefore be ye also ready: for in such an hour as ye think not, the Son of man cometh.' In those hours when we think salvation is never coming; when we hurt too much to be ready to receive holy redemption; when our heart is weary, and our grief is heavy on our shoulders; in the darkest of those hours, do not despair. When one of us is taken in senseless violence, like our brother Orrin Wilkins, do not stray from God's side. The Son of God is on his way! In our lifetime, Judgment Day shall come, and we true believers shall be taken home to our creator. All our sins will be forgiven, even the most heinous of them, because our faith is true. And Orrin Wilkins will be there to welcome us home."

I turned around and left. The rain was better than this. A lecture on the Rapture was the last thing I needed right now. I needed some TLC from my gal Sal.

CHAPTER THIRTY-FOUR

Unfortunately, when I got to her house, I had to get through a very angry Heather. Sally had already dumped on me, but Heather was in Brawley the night I released Justin into Tara's custody.

"You're such a wuss, Warren. How dare you take Justin away! All your sister has to do is say jump, and you're halfway over the candlestick. You've got to go over there right now and bring him back!"

They had been trimming their tree. It was the first tree I'd ever seen with chains of safety pins, strings of dried noodles, and a brooding, fuzzy vulture on the top. But when she saw me, Heather turned from a Goth Martha Stewart into Godzilla. Now it was "Warren roasting on an open fire" and I knew I wasn't going to get a lot of help from Sally.

I waded in. "I miss the little bugger too, Heather. But my sister's right. Justin knew her. I watched him give her this huge smile when he saw her. Besides, she has a lot more experience raising kids and lion cubs. She loves animals, and right now Justin is more animal than person . . ."

I watched Heather's face harden up. Oops, wrong track! "I mean, she just knows what she's doing. And she can give him twenty-four/seven care, instead of us jury-rigging together a coverage schedule. Heather, it comes down to this: what's best for Justin. His dad is dead; his mom is in the hospital and headed for jail. He needs someone familiar around him who can be totally dedicated to him. Not a girl still in high school, a woman who spends most of her day in front of a computer screen, and a street vendor. The person Justin needs is Tara. Sorry, but you know it's true."

She sighed. "I still don't like it."

"Me neither. But we can go over and visit any time we want. And I'm sure Tara will want us to do some babysitting after a while. We're all still family."

She nodded, reluctantly, and went back to putting black balls on the tree.

Sally came over. "Nice job. You're getting pretty good at this dad thing."

"I'm ready to retire, though. Do you mind if I just download all over you?"

"Come on outside."

We went out to the back deck, overlooking the hills. When the sun was up you could see a bit of the Sacramento River from here. But now the stars were out, a river of white splashed across the sky. All that rain stayed south of us.

I talked about Fran, the sci-fi writer, Vespie, Lorraine, Judgment Day, and my gay old man. I hadn't planned to share that part right away, but like Rose said, I had no impulse control. It just blurted out. Sally was bisexual, so it wasn't such a big-deal story for her.

I thought about going out and getting the letter for her to read, but it seemed like too far to walk. I started to feel the weariness of this day.

After a while there was nothing left to say. We were quiet. There was one victorious screech from a bird of prey flying somewhere over our heads. We could hear the river wind as it blew toward Sacramento, rustling the bare branches of the oaks on its journey eastward. Then just the quiet darkness. The night began to soak up my tension. I sat there, relishing the silence.

I pointed to a star that flashed red and white. "That's Sirius. I had an English teacher in eighth grade. She made us memorize poems. One of my favorites was about that star. I mean, I pretend that it was. I decided Browning was looking at the same star."

"Do you still remember it?"

"Sure, I think so."

> All that I know
>> Of a certain star
> Is, it can throw
>> (Like the angled spar)
> Now a dart of red,
>> Now a dart of blue;
> Till my friends have said
>> They would fain see, too,
> My star that dartles the red and the blue!
> Then it stops like a bird; like a flower hangs furled:
>> They must solace themselves with the Saturn above it.
> What matter to me if their star is a world?
>> Mine has opened its soul to me, therefore I love it.

Sally sighed. "Nice. I like it when poems rhyme. It's too bad we all got too sophisticated for that."

I said, "You know, a funny thing happened when Fran showed up at my table last week. One of the cards dropped out of my deck. It was the Star card. That didn't make much sense at the time, but now I'm beginning to understand."

"What's it mean?"

"It's about life purpose, about having a sense of purpose. My dad kept denying his truth until he had to break everything apart to reclaim it. Fran lost her reason for living, and just wanted to die. I think I buried mine for years, just keeping on the run and under everybody's radar. But I think I'm starting to find mine. This fatherhood thing, it's got to me. I really want to save my girl."

Sally took my hand. "Warren, you've been a runner your whole life. Trying to reverse that in just a year must be hell. But, you hang in there. There's a lot more riding on you being able to commit than you can see. Heather is watching you to see if men can be trusted. Fran is waiting to find out if she really has a father. Tara is slowly beginning to trust you. Justin is going to form a lot of what he knows about how to be a man from your relationship with him. And I want to love you. I bet that must feel pretty claustrophobic sometimes, all those eyes on you."

I nodded.

"In the sixties you were fighting the wrong fight, Warren. This year you are fighting the right one. We've opened our souls to you. Don't let us down."

"I won't."

We got real quiet. Sally finally said, "OK, let's see if any of the stuff I found out today helps save Fran's butt. I've got interesting news, and bad news. First the interesting stuff. I got a fragment from the last week of the files Orrin was keeping for Homeland Security."

"Hey, I thought you were scared of messing with the Feds."

"Now I am, that's for sure. I nearly got my ass fried. But you know me. I just wanted to see if I could pull it off. When the government vans pull up, you'll know I failed. But I don't think that's going to happen. Anyway, I didn't stay long, and I didn't get much. Just one memo. He reported that he'd uncovered an outstanding murder warrant for one of the people in the group he had penetrated. He didn't mention any names, but he mentioned that he thought he could use this information to turn the person into an informant. I couldn't get any more, because I was getting back-traced pretty heavily. I got out just in time. That's definitely the last time I mess with them!"

I said, "And Levar was at the funeral. How can we find out if he's our man?"

"A fingerprint might be nice."

I tipped Levar/Lawrence's card out of my wallet and onto her lap. "Here you go."

Sally took an envelope from a side pocket of her chair and carefully nudged the card inside.

Then her smile faded. "Now the bad news. On Monday, they're going to move Fran from the hospital to the jail."

"Ouch. That means I have two days to catch this guy?"

"Afraid so. And you want to keep the stuff about your dad's death on hold?"

"Please, just for now."

Just then Heather called, "OK, you guys, come on in!"

We entered a room that was dark except for the tree, trimmed in tiny red lights with a rung of white lights at the top that illuminated the Christmas Buzzard.

We simultaneously said, "Ooh, it's beautiful!"

A phone message was waiting for me when I got home, but I was just too tired. I crashed hard.

SATURDAY, DECEMBER 24

And in despair I bowed my head:
"There is no peace on earth," I said,
"For hate is strong and mocks the song
Of peace on earth, good will to men."

—"I Heard the Bells on Christmas Day,"
Henry W. Longfellow

CHAPTER THIRTY-FIVE

Saturday morning: The birds were singing for some godforsaken reason, since the rain had finally made its way up to Berkeley. The bells on campus were playing Satie's "Three Gymnopedies." And the axe blade was slowly descending on my daughter's neck. I had two days to keep her out of the slammer. Somehow I felt that, once she was behind bars, there would be no hope. Whatever had to be done, today was the day to do it.

Step one was to listen to my message. No wait, step one was to kickstart my mental engine. I grabbed my poncho and made a quick trip across the street. That provided me with a bathtub-sized container of barely drinkable coffee, today's paper, and three coconut-covered doughnuts. (Everybody knows the rules: Maple bars are for depression, coconut is for focus, and bran muffins are for losers who think eating 350 calories is a path toward health.)

I wolfed and gulped until my mind crawled out of the swamp on stubby legs. After regaining the capacity to read, I browsed through news of war, starvation, pollution, and positive financial forecasts. I was looking to see if there was any more information about Fran's case, but it was another name that jumped off the page.

HIGHTOWER-McFERRON

Julia Hightower and Jason McFerron are pleased to announce their engagement.

The bride-to-be is the daughter of the late Don and Louise Hightower of Portland, Maine. She received her bachelor's degree from UCLA in 1991.

The groom-to-be is the son of David and Mary McFerron of Walnut Creek. He earned his Ph.D. in chemical engineering from Cal Poly in 1952. Jason is employed as a Senior Computational Biologist at Lawrence Berkeley National Laboratory.

Julia and Jason met while vacationing on Fiji. A January wedding is planned.

She was at it again: older guy, mythical parents. Well, we had until January to stop her. First things first: save my daughter.

I hit the play button. It was my favorite cop on a trike. Mac sounded like he'd been scraped off those cliffs he had been thrashing. "Oh, man, I'm hurting, Warren. God, I'm tired. We nearly got killed on those rocks when the rains hit.

"OK, so I talked with Sam, my biker friend on the Santa Cruz force. Where to start? According to Sam, Orrin Wilkins, presently deceased, was a major climber. He glad-handed everyone in sight, did some righteous busts, and was angling to go to law school, in the hopes of eventually becoming a Fed. Orrin was doing an undercover stint with the San Jose police to kiss up to Homeland Security folks and get noticed. In fact, there's a rumor making the rounds that he'd been offered a training instructor's job at the Federal Law Enforcement Training Center in Georgia at double the salary he's making now.

"Bottom line, a good guy to have covering your back in a fire-fight, but he'd knife you to advance his career. Smiling faces, and all that. Everybody thinks his wife popped him.

"Ted Vespie was old school. Busted heads, and enforced his version of the law. Not great on customer relations. Just got back from vacation two weeks ago to find out he was a target of Internal Affairs, and word is that Wilkins dropped a dime on him. But that's just a rumor. Sam kind of doubted it, since Vespie was so torn up over Wilkins's death. They were partners for years. Vespie got pulled off the Wilkins homicide because he was going postal trying to find out who did it. That's what I know. What the hell are you doing in the middle of this mess? I hope it doesn't have anything to do with Mrs. Wilkins, because she's going down for this one. Call me."

Great. I was so glad Mac had reported in. This was looking completely hopeless now. I could feel my depression cresting. Maybe I was going to need those maple bars after all. While I sat there contemplating future pastry choices the phone rang. It was Sally.

"Good morning, Travis McGee. How's it going?"

"Not too good, Doctor Watson. I don't know what to do next."

"Well, here's another chunk to toss into the chipper. It took all night, but I got it. Those prints you gave me came up positive for a ten-year-old homicide in Texas. A black guy killed a sheriff's deputy. The case is still open. And right now some secretary in Minnesota is trying to figure out why the Galveston Police

171

Department is calling them about a thumb print that no one in Minneapolis remembers entering into the IAFIS."

"Thanks, Sally. Give me the Los Gatos address on Levar's card. I guess it's time to make a home visit. Oh, and I want one more address, too. Tell me where Ms. Hightower currently resides. I think it's time I met my evil stepmother. Then, go check out page B-4 of today's *Chronicle*."

CHAPTER THIRTY-SIX

At first I thought that the killing-off-old-guys business must be paying pretty well. Julia lived in a modern, post-firestorm mansion hanging near the top of the Oakland Hills. If the sky weren't gray and foreboding, the view would have been glorious. The house looked down on the Bay Area like the gods must have looked down on Greece from Mount Olympus. Then I remembered the newly engaged couple was already living together in sin. These were probably the biologist's digs.

This mansion was on the more expensive, downhill side of Grizzly Peak. Most of the house lay below the front door, cascading down from terrace to terrace.

I knocked on the front door, and an attractive, pixy-like blonde opened it—glittery sapphire eyes, and a face with the finest filigree of wrinkles. She was of indeterminate age, and might be the Queen of the Fairies on growth hormone.

I tried, "Julia Hightower?"

"Yes?"

No wonder she was good at this job. She had that geisha stop-you-with-one-look ability of gazing at you as if you were the most interesting man in the world.

"I'd like to talk with you about your father, Dr. Higgins."

Bam! The door slammed so hard I almost got a concussion from the shock wave. I knocked again, to no avail. Then I went back to my car, carefully hidden in a turnout down the road, and waited. If all that crappy TV I watched as a kid was good for anything, then soon she'd come zooming out and unknowingly lead me to her father.

An hour later I decided it was time to stop watching TV. I headed for Los Gatos.

CHAPTER THIRTY-SEVEN

As I drove through the drizzle, I thought about my approach to crime-busting. I'd read voraciously: *Forensics for Dummies, The Complete Idiot's Guide to Private Investigating, The Criminal Mind,* and *The Law Enforcement Handbook.* They all said the same thing: When you're dealing with homicide, go get a policeman. Don't mess with a murderer. Great advice, but what happens when the murderer might just be the policeman? Vespie was high on my list of suspects.

I didn't have a Sherlockian mind that could sift all the evidence until finally I was ready to expose Colonel Mustard in the library. I'm not as tough as Spencer or as ruthless as Jack Reacher. And besides, those are all fictional characters. No real person in their right mind would go after a murderer alone, let alone two separate murderers. Ah, but that's where I had the advantage over everyone else. I wasn't in my right mind. In fact I didn't even have a right mind. The advantage of being a whack job is that there is very little common sense to warn me off.

So I was off to do what I do best: piss off enough people so that one of them makes a bonehead mistake. Then try not to get killed. It had worked fabulously well the first time this spring. It blew up in my face this fall. My lovely interaction with Ms. Hightower this morning was a classic example of how well this approach didn't work. Well, to paraphrase Scarlett, "This afternoon's another day!"

Levar lived in a postage-stamp-sized Victorian gardener's cottage off the main drag. He did drive a Camry. It was parked right in front. Time to go turn a friend into an enemy.

I knocked. Levar checked me out through the peephole and then opened the door. "What are you doing out there in this weather, Traveler?"

"You don't want to talk about this on your front stoop, Levar. Let me in."

He didn't like it. I didn't like it. But there I was, seated on his futon couch while he brought me a San Miguel Dark. Screw my medication. It was too early for a beer, but today was going to suck, anyway; I might as well do it with a buzz. See what I mean about common sense?

His pad looked transitory. Brick-and-board bookcases, a dining room set from Cost Plus, nothing remarkably personal, except a magnificent blue marlin that arched across one wall. He settled into his red Naugahyde Barcalounger, sipped his coffee, and waited.

I took a long pull. Then, "You were lying to me at the pool hall. I don't blame you for not being straight with me. There's lots that I've done that I keep hidden, too. Not telling me about the cop in Texas was understandable. But holding back on what happened between you and Orrin on the night he was shot sucks. Did you kill him?"

Not the slightest change in expression. This guy was good.

"Traveler, you've been a busy man. And you're right, what happened in Texas is none of your business. Even though I'm sure the black neighborhoods of Galveston would gladly put up a statue in my honor for offing that racist Texas Ranger. To answer your question, no. I didn't kill Oscar, or Orrin as you know him."

I was firing into the dark. "You knew he was a cop. He was going to turn you in."

Levar leaned forward and looked straight at me. I could see in his face that, finally, I was going to get the straight dope.

"We were at the same pool hall where you and I ate. It was a couple days before he got plugged. Over beers he said, in a voice as casual as though he were talking about the Super Bowl, 'So Lawrence, or should I call you Levar?'

"I kept my cool. I said, 'Levar?'

"He grinned, 'Levar? Lebna? Don't pounce, Mr. Panther. We've got some dealing to do. I know all about Texas.'

"I knew right then that I was fucked. I didn't say a word. Oscar went on, 'Don't worry, I'm not a Fed. What happened down south, or back in Chicago, is of no interest to me whatsoever. You play the game with me, and that information stays buried.

"'I'm just a local cop trying to make a name for myself. Enlightened self-interest, you may have heard of that? I got on this undercover gig to help me make the jump out of the street and into more interesting work. The FBI is a waste. Too many protocols, educational requirements, background checks, mental health screenings, and all that crap.

"'But Homeland Security . . . now that's the land of golden opportunity. All you need is a willingness to get results. Are you with me here, Lawrence?'

"All I did was nod.

"Then he said something like, 'Which brings me to this evening's discussion. Well, monologue really, since I don't yet require an answer. We both have similar aims. You want to keep your nice comfortable life in your secure new identity. I want to find me a terrorist, so I can move up and get out of your nappy hair.

" 'Those bingo-headed peaceniks at the South Bay Force for Freedom couldn't fight their way out of a trail mix bag. But, with your help, we're going to nail one of them with direct links to Al Qaeda. I don't care who, you get to pick. But one of them is going down. And don't worry, I'm not going to need you to testify or anything. We'll just send them to Guantanamo. There's no need for a trial. I get the credit for the catch, and you get left alone. Sound good?'

"Nappy my ass. This guy totally pissed me off. I said, 'Of course I don't know what you are talking about.'

"He wasn't buying it. He said, 'Hey, don't worry. I'm not carrying a wire. Anyway, this is just a meeting to sound you out. You don't have to do anything at this point. I'll be back later with the details.

" 'But if you are thinking about blowing the whistle about me to your little 'Give peace a chance' scout troop back there, be prepared to go to the chair in Texas. I am monitoring your bank accounts and I have surveillance on you twenty-four/seven. If you make the slightest move to split, I will have you behind bars so fast you won't know what hit you. *Capisce*?'

"Sure, I'm going to believe he's not wired? No way. I told him, 'You are making no sense to me whatsoever, Oscar.'

"Dumb little shit said something like, 'Right on, bro. Let me buy you another round.' Then he called out to the waitress, 'Hey honey, two Maker's Marks over here. We're celebrating! Get me a little plastered and then you can clean me out on the pool table, right?'

"I was so over this snake. I told him, 'Listen, Oscar, or whatever your name is, I prefer neither to drink with nor play pool with a running-dog scum. Thank you for this entertaining evening. When you go home to your den, I hope your mother bites you and gives you rabies. Good night.'

"As I was walking away, he said, 'I'll talk to you in a couple of weeks. You be careful out there.' "

So that was the story. There was one more question I had to ask. "So did you cooperate?"

"Hell no! He wanted to turn me into his little stoolie. He was a very ambitious man. He called me the night he died to set up a time for us to move into the next phase of the operation. After that call, I decided to get my ass out of here before he could fuck with me. But then he did me the favor of getting killed."

I shook my head. "You sound guilty to me, Levar. Any alibi for that night?"

"Traveler, do you really think I'm stupid enough to off an undercover cop? I've already killed that guy in Chicago and that murderous pig in Texas. Two cop killings, hell, I wouldn't even make it to the lethal injection. The Man would shoot me down in the street. Alibi, hell no. I was home, packing. Getting ready to go on the run again."

I remembered what that empty feeling of getting ready to pull up stakes felt like. I knew in my gut he didn't kill Orrin. He'd never give me that perfect a motive if he was guilty. I finished off my beer and got up. "Thanks for the drink. I just want you to know one thing. If I find out you did it, I'll make sure it's you, and not my daughter, who does the time. You understand?"

"I get it. You're her dad. But I didn't do it. I'm not that stupid. Not anymore. Just don't try to hang anything on me to save her butt. Payback will be a major bitch for you if you play that game."

He was damn serious.

"Hang it on the black man? No, Levar, you know me better than that. Whatever I do, it will be face to face, and there won't be any bullshit involved."

He held out his hand. I shook it, and hoped to hell he wasn't the one.

CHAPTER THIRTY-EIGHT

Next, it was time to take on Christianity. Down I went to the seventh canto of Santa Cruz. I drove to the address on Rev. Dalton's card. Lorraine met me at the front door in a long floral dress, slit nicely up the side. "You're Fran's father, right? It's nice to see you again. I'm sorry, Larry's over at the church, decorating. Is there anything I can do? It's pouring out there. Would you like to come in?"

Nice people. Didn't she read fem-jep, sexist, exploitive, serial killer novels? I could have a butcher knife hidden behind my back. Which reminded me, way too late, that I should have brought my Beretta .32 along. Ah, well.

"Yes, you might be able to help me, Lorraine. Thanks."

I walked into a cool, open living room decorated with a tropical theme: Turquoise, yellow, and lime green throw pillows graced the chairs and the couch. The upholstery had a matching pattern of island flowers. The end tables were white rattan, and a whitewashed coffee table had a display of polished shells under its transparent surface. Several shells were on top of the glass. I picked up a lovely small purple one to examine. Lorraine called into the hallway and soon a young Hispanic girl brought a tray with two drinks on it. The lemonade matched the color scheme perfectly.

She turned to her maid. "Thank you, Rita." Then she looked at me. "Well, I see you're admiring my collection. That's the shell of a fragile violet snail. I just brought it back from my last trip."

She crossed those legs and sipped her drink. Not suggestive, just damn elegant.

"Did you collect all these?"

"Every one. I waste every vacation underwater. It's a sport I can do with three limbs." She smiled and looked down at her left arm. "I have to use a ton of sunscreen, but I love the islands. So how is Fran doing?"

A swimmer's body, definitely.

"Fran's back among the living, but I'm scared that she is going to end up in jail for a murder she didn't commit. I'm trying to help her. Actually I could use your help, if you don't mind. You knew them; they were both in your church. What was your impression of Fran?"

She sighed faintly. "Fran was a troubled person. I was worried about her, and about Justin. I hope you don't mind me saying this?"

"Oh no, I know a lot about her struggles, believe me. Go on."

"Well, at times she was in the center of church affairs, organizing, cleaning, throwing herself into service. A real delight. Then suddenly, she would just disappear. And she seemed so sad when she resurfaced. It was odd."

Odd indeed. Sounded just like my lifestyle, take away the church activities. "And what did you think about Orrin?"

Had it gotten suddenly colder in here? Tiny, etched lines emerged on Lorraine's porcelain face. Then they were gone. "Up until recently, Orrin was an active member of the governing body of our church. He will be missed."

I had the distinct impression that she was about to, very politely, toss me back into the deluge. I remembered a similar response from her back in the hospital room. Orrin was definitely a conversation stopper for her. I headed her off before she could throw me out by asking to use her lavatory. "Down the hall, the second door on the left."

No serious drugs in the medicine chest or the drawers. On the way back to the living room I gently pushed open the doors: a guest bedroom, and then what must be the good reverend's study. No hint of Hawaii here: on the walls a nice collection of stuffed heads of North American mammals (*Homo sapiens* noticeably missing), a massive walnut rolltop desk (closed), a gun cabinet, and the pelt of some creature on the floor. I sensed, rather than heard, her presence by my side.

"My husband is an avid hunter. He'd often go out with Orrin and Ted Vespie. I'm sure he counted Orrin as a special friend. He's at the church and can answer your questions far better than I could."

I let her start to escort me to the front door, but I was going to get as many questions in as I could before she whisked me out. I asked the one I most dreaded to hear answered.

"Do you think Fran is capable of murder?"

"I have no magical cards to consult to help me understand the motivations of other people, or predict the outcome of their actions, Mr. Ritter. I'm a simple minister's wife, and I really couldn't tell you what she could do. Under the right circumstances, I imagine anyone is capable of murder. It was nice seeing you again."

One handshake and I was dismissed. Then I was facing a closed door. Well, that was very interesting! Time to go to church.

CHAPTER THIRTY-NINE

I found Dalton with a gaggle of devout interior decorators, tacking garlands around the gray corners of that forbidding church. It was kind of like livening up a sepulchre, but I admired their panache. Dalton was on the top of an ancient stepladder hanging a glittering star over a giant wreath. I called up, "Reverend, I need to speak with you for a moment, if that's all right."

He smiled beatifically down at me. "Sure, no problem. Let me finish this and I'll be right down."

He climbed down and wiped his hands on his pants. "Follow me."

We went through a door in back of the sanctuary. Then we walked through a narrow vestry and opened another door into a short hallway. One leg of the hall ended in an exit. We headed the other way. Dalton ushered me into his office.

The masculine club atmosphere that I noticed in his study continued here. Two oversized brown leather chairs were positioned in front of a small fireplace. Behind them tall bookshelves crammed full of significant-looking volumes lined the walls. A big cherry wood desk dominated one end. Underneath everything was a vast, thick, Oriental rug. No dead animals looking down on us, though.

"Can I offer you anything to drink, a Coke or water, or something stronger?"

I was going to be afloat if all my suspects were this generous. "No thank you." We nestled into those enfolding chairs.

"Reverend, you know that my daughter has been accused of murdering her husband."

"You can call me Larry. Of course I heard about that. Is there any way I can help?"

"I'm trying to find out if she did it. If she didn't, I want to know who did."

"Isn't that the job of the police?"

Civilians. So trusting of authority. He probably votes Republican, too, in spite of being gay. "Actually, the police have already made up their minds on the matter. All they're doing right now is gathering more evidence for the prosecutor's office." And suppressing or destroying any evidence that might contradict their earnestly held beliefs. But I didn't say this. I didn't want Larry to think I might be a radical or anything scary like that.

"Oh, I think that's a little harsh."

See what I mean? Police are good, criminals are bad, terrorists have tons of weapons of mass destruction, and corporations are our friends. The comfortable delusions of a civilization on the brink of collapse. But this was not the time to proselytize.

"You may be right, Larry. But l have a couple of questions that might set my mind at ease."

"Go ahead."

He'd be sorry he said that. "Did Orrin threaten to expose you when he found out you beat up your lover, Dean Pak?"

In the arena of keeping one's cool, Levar had this guy beaten hands down. Larry's face turned beet red, his fists balled up, and I thought he was getting ready to spring on top of me and give us a repeat of L.A. "You little prick, who do you think you are?"

"Reverend! Cool your jets here, dude. 'Gay Minister Assaults Bereaved Father'? That's going to make a disastrous headline on the front page of tomorrow's *Sentinel*. Now, sit back down!"

He did, barely.

"What the fuck do you want?"

Boy, self-control had flown out the window. "Look, I don't give a rat's behind what your sexual preference is. Just answer my question. I know Orrin confided in you. I also want to know if he was threatening you."

"No."

"Hmmm, I wonder if you could be a little more forthcoming. Honestly, I'm not going to 'out' you. I really don't want to cause you grief. I'm just trying to find out who killed my late son-in-law. Besides, I think you might want to talk about what happened the night he died."

Someone opened the nozzle, and all the hot air that had inflated him was let out. He slumped, and then said, "It wasn't the night he died. It was a few weeks before. We were closer than you'd think. Orrin and I were good friends. Or so I thought. He had known I was gay for a long time. But he didn't know about Dean.

"Well, he and I were having a boys' night out drinking. We did this at least once a month. Sometimes Vespie would join us, but that night it was just the two of us, drinking boilermakers in Watsonville, far from my congregation.

"It was one of those pseudocowboy bars. The bartender wore a bandana and most of the drinkers were in well-pressed designer blue jeans. Not one person in the place had ever had one of his full-quill ostrich skin boots in a stirrup. They drank, flirted, and listened to songs about lonely truckers and heartbroken good women.

"I had a couple too many. That often happened in these gatherings. Orrin, though, was still nursing his first beer, so he could drive me back home.

"I said to him, 'You seem awfully quiet this evening.'

"That's when it all started to unravel. He said, 'Actually I think I am having a crisis of faith, Dalton. And it's all about you.'

"I had no idea what he was talking about. I said something like, 'I'm not sure what you mean.'

"He said, 'Well, you know, your being gay and keeping it a secret has been hard on me. Sure, I've helped out, and covered for you. But it just leaves a bad taste in my mouth, pardon the pun.'

"I hated that he might be talking about that in public. Orrin noticed my fear. 'Don't worry, I'm not going to out you tonight. But I still haven't decided what to do with what I just learned.'

"I still was lost. 'What you just learned? I don't understand what you're talking about.'

"He said, 'I know you beat the shit out of Dean Pak.'

"I began to sweat. I asked him how he found out.

"He stood up. 'I'm a cop, remember. I just ran across the information a couple of days ago. So you beat the crap out of an ex-lover and then scared him into not pressing charges. This is the man I trust my salvation with? You're a thug, a pervert, and a liar. And I should just go before the Board of Governors and tell them what kind of minister they sent out to guide us.'

"I needed him to shut up. I said, 'Orrin? I thought you were my friend.'

"He glared at me for a long time. He looked pissed, but I wondered if he was secretly enjoying how frightened he made me feel. Then he said, 'A friend would tell a friend about their bloody past and not keep secrets from him. But you're nothing but secrets, aren't you, Dalton? Drive yourself home tonight, I'm taking a cab.'

"I thought he was going to broadcast it all over Santa Cruz. But he didn't. He just never came back to church, and never spoke to me again."

I thought I'd throw in my two pfennig. "Actually, from everything I've learned about the guy, I think he delighted in every moment he spent scaring the piss out of you. I've never heard of a man more in need of killing."

Dalton still didn't trust me. He said, "So tell me what you're up to. Are you going to 'out' me, just to get Fran freed?"

I shrugged. "Not if you didn't do it. Look, I don't know who killed Orrin. Maybe Fran did it. Maybe you did it. I just don't know. If Fran shot him, then I'll let her go do her time. But if you killed him, I will bring you down."

He nodded. "Fair enough. Now will you please get the hell out of here, so I can go back to work."

As we got up, I tried the old Colombo thing. "Did you ever get to read Fran's suicide note?"

"No. Good-bye."

"One last thing. You're gay but you're married. How does that work?"

"None of your damn business. Now get out."

That doorknob strategy worked so well for Peter Falk.

CHAPTER FORTY

The next suspect sure wasn't going to offer me anything to drink. I headed for the hospital. The cop in front of her door was reluctant to let me in, but eventually he checked his list and relented. Fran sat up in her bed, typing on her laptop. She looked up and smiled weakly at me. Her skin looked bleached. Her black hair stuck out in all directions; her eyes still had that haunted look of a refugee from a prison camp. But she smiled. This was huge progress.

I pulled up a chair. "Hi, sweetie. How're you feeling?"

"Like a fecal milkshake. How about you?"

Hey, she asked about me! She *was* feeling better. "I'm pretty lost right now. I'm trying to find out who killed Orrin, but I'm not having much luck."

"I hear they're moving me over to the jail Monday. I guess I should be thankful they let me have Christmas in this godforsaken place. It must beat jail."

I wish they hadn't told her. But I wished a lot of things. It didn't seem to make any difference. "Let me tell you about today.

Maybe you can see something I can't." So I told her the story of my encounter with Levar, heavily abridged and leaving out all our past history. She had no comment. Then I told her the story of Lorraine and lemonade. All she said was, "Yeah, it's funny. It's been days since I've talked with her. Lorraine stopped coming over, or even answering my phone calls. I thought I could count on her when things got tough, but I think she just crossed me off her list. I mean, a lot of people do that, but usually I know why they do it. I still don't have a clue about her."

I wouldn't tell her about Dalton's violence toward his ex-boyfriend. It wouldn't be fair to him or to her. So I said, "Tell me about Orrin."

She turned away and mumbled something.

I asked, "What?"

"I said you wouldn't believe me."

"On the contrary, I would very much believe you. Here's what I already know: He was a snake, a manipulator, and a toad who would arrest his mother to go up a grade at work. Am I far off?"

She turned back to me, her eyes sad and weary. "Yes, as a matter of fact you are off. You have woefully underestimated him. He was the most evil man I ever met. He would charm you, listen to every word, remember the smallest details of your life, and make love slowly, sensuously, and ever so attuned to your needs."

This was more detail than I wanted, but I just listened.

"With men, he learned what gave them hidden pride, and played those keys like a maestro. With other women he flattered in such a subtle way you would never think he was being seductive. In a crowded room, wherever the laughter was, Orrin was in the center of it. Yet he wasn't telling jokes or entertaining. He just made everyone around him feel special.

"And it was all done so that they ended up needing his attention, just a little more each time. He was always looking for the key, the one thing that could destroy you. Because, in truth, he didn't give a damn about anyone but Orrin. He only enjoyed one thing. When the time was right he would give the subtle hint, the gentle shove toward your destruction. As you sank lower into your self-made pit, he watched and listened. He was so very sympathetic as he guided you into destroying your life.

"He got Reverend Dalton to drink too much. He pushed Teddy Vespie to knock suspects around too much. He had me feeling like I was the worst mother that ever lived. I thought the only person he couldn't corrupt was Lorraine, but I guess he got to her in the end, too."

She went silent. I said, "I hear that he wanted to become a Homeland Security agent. Sounds like a career that would have suited him well."

She shook her head. "He fed off fear. I think he wanted to end up the president of the United States. Then he could terrorize the whole nation from within. It would be a great sport for him."

She reached out and grabbed my arm. "Warren, I haven't gotten to the worst part, that would happen when he was done playing with you. Then he would just abuse you. Never so that anyone could find a bruise. But he would just treat you like an inanimate object that he used and discarded. Only you never dared speak about it. Because, by that time, he had enough to ruin you. I was so afraid of what he was going to do to Justin. He deserved death ten times over."

"Not so loud, Fran. They might have this place wired for sound."

"I don't care, really." She sank lower in her bed.

I dropped my voice to a whisper. With all the machinery around her it was going to be damn hard for them to pick anything up. "I hate to ask this, but I've got to know. Did you kill him, Fran? And please answer very softly. I don't want this conversation ending up in court."

There was a long silence.

I could barely hear her. "I don't know. I was out drinking like a water buffalo that night. Teddy says there is no one that can alibi me after eleven. I don't remember a damn thing."

"Vespie would tell you that he saw you fire the gun if he could get away with it."

"Was it his own gun?"

"I think so."

Another long sigh. "I don't know what's real and what's fantasy. I imagined a thousand times just emptying a clip from that gun into him. I can almost see myself doing it. But I don't know if I did or not. Sorry, Dad, I can't help you. But you can help me."

"Sure, anything."

"They are sending a shrink over here to evaluate me in a few minutes. I guess they want to decide if I am still a suicide risk, or something. Anyway I need some help conning him into believing I'm OK."

"You know, I can get a lawyer down here and stop all this garbage right in its tracks."

"I'd rather get a clean bill of health. Who knows, maybe someday I'll be out of here. I don't want some crappy diagnosis following me around."

I flipped open my cell phone. "I've got just the ticket." Then I pushed a button on the side and spoke "Rose" into it.

CHAPTER FORTY-ONE

I t was dark and raining by the time I got on Highway 17 and headed north. Fran told me Rose had been reluctant at first, but finally got into it and the two of them had an animated half hour together. Fran actually laughed a few times. Then the hospital shrink showed up. My daughter had given me a kiss as I left. God, I hoped I could keep that girl out of prison!

There were just too many tangled connections, most of them bogus: sailfish, shell collections, ministers with gun racks, alien flowers, memories, delusions, and one very pissed-off cop who swore in pidgin. There must be a common thread, but I was damned if I could see it.

This road was a bitch to drive even when the weather was dry, and now it was worse. Besides, I was getting hungry. All I'd had today was doughnuts, caffeine, lemonade, and beer. I was trying to figure out how to get to the Cats Restaurant from this side of the highway when I noticed out of the side of my vision a white panel truck pull up parallel to me. I glanced over in time to see, in the glint of headlights, the barrel of a very large rifle aimed right at me.

I tromped down on the accelerator, swerved the wheel, tried to duck down (damn seatbelt!), and then I heard the loudest noise I had ever heard. Glass peppered me. My car flew off the road, into brush, and then slammed into a tree, shattering the windshield. The back of my head and my right shoulder burned like acid. Blood covered the steering wheel.

CHAPTER FORTY-TWO

It was weird. A part of me lay jammed against the steering wheel screaming and bleeding, as the smell of gunpowder and raw gasoline gagged me. Another part just popped right out and watched calmly, neutrally, in a spot about twenty feet above the scene of the wreck.

I watched as a pickup pulled over and a lady talked frantically on her cell phone. After a while I began to hear sirens. Police cars came in from both directions of the freeway and congregated at my car. I watched two cops pulling out a Jaws of Life saw. Then my old friend Teddy Vespie ran over to the car, yelling, "Hell, there's no time for that. Besides, you don't need that, it's just a Honda!"

There was gas on the ground around him as he grabbed the door that wedged me in and bent the window frame sideways. Then he reached in and grabbed me by the shoulders. In a soft voice only I could hear, he said, "Warren. I should have known. Hope your back ain't broken." Then he hauled my blood-soaked body out of the car and dragged me away. The part of me that was down there in my body screamed. The other part of me just floated above, curious and unattached. When we were about ten feet away from the wreck, just like in the movies, the car went "whump!" and turned into a flaming pyre in the rain.

Teddy called out, "First-aid kit, this guy's been shot." Then the ambulance attendants pushed Vespie aside, bandaged the back of my head and my shoulders, and hooked me up to IVs. When they strapped me down to a board, I was sucked down like a vacuum cleaner back into my body. I started screaming again. I'd never felt pain like that before.

I was lying in Coast Memorial Emergency when Sally came wheeling in. "Goddamn it, Warren, I told you not to get shot at this time!"

You know, getting your head blown off and then crashing your car really sucks. I didn't need her attitude on top of that. But she didn't look angry. She looked very frightened. She was pale, and her eyes were red, and very big. OK, self-management time. "Sorry, baby, I guess I messed up royally this time. The docs tell me it was number seven shot. That's a whole lot of hurt, but at least I'm still alive! So far no whiplash, or broken bones or anything."

"Until I kill you."

"Yeah, well, I think I'd rather you did it. It's more personal that way. How did you get here?"

She smiled, and already the pain started to diminish. OK, the morphine helped a little, too. But not all that much. The back of my head still felt like someone was pressing it against a red-hot burner.

"You have me listed in your wallet as the person to contact in an emergency."

I remembered doing that last month. It was the first time I'd ever filled out one of those cards. I guess I was finally setting down roots. Rather bloody roots, at the moment.

"Sally, I'm damn glad you're here. I've got work for you to do. I need you to contact Max. I want to get somebody inside Reverend Dalton's house."

Max was an old friend of Sally's and a new friend of mine. He ran Valdez Security Systems, a rather unique organization that could provide you a bodyguard, a surveillance team, a spy, or maybe even a hit man. Most of his operatives were illegal immigrants. He claimed that they were invisible, because white people never noticed the Hispanics who do the jobs that hold up the backbone of the white man's world.

"What do you need?"

"There's a gun cabinet with glass doors in his study. I think I noticed a pump-action shotgun in it. I want someone to check the barrel and tell me if it's been fired recently. They might be able to smell it. I don't know. It's just a shot; pardon my pun."

"I'll get on it. Now I think you need to lie back down and rest. Looks like you'll be spending Christmas right here."

"You know, Sally, when I thought about spending Christmas with my daughter this wasn't quite what I had in mind. There's one more thing I need you to do."

"You're beginning to bug me, Warren. Stop thinking and rest!"

"OK, I will. Just let me ask one thing, and I promise I'll shut up. Can you access your files from here?"

"Don't be stupid. Of course."

"OK, then, I want you to send an e-mail to Jason McFerron, that biologist fiancé of Julia Hightower. Send it to him at his Lawrence Berkeley Labs address. Tell him everything we know about Julia and her dad, but don't mention my father by name. Then say something like this, 'Dr. McFerron, you're a scientist. Just answer these three questions and you'll discover whether this is a crackpot e-mail or a true warning. One, did Julia refuse to sign a prenuptial agreement? Two, did she recently get you to see an elderly cardiologist named Dr. Higgins? Three, are you a bit surprised that a woman so much younger than you is so amazingly interested in you? If you come up with some 'yes' answers, you are in grave danger. Please contact the police.' Sign it 'Hamlet's protégé.'"

Sally sighed. "I just hope it wasn't Julia or her dad in that van, because he could waltz right in here and give you one of his special fake heart attacks. I'm going to get Max to post someone outside your door, and I'm not leaving until he gets here."

"Thanks, Sally. The thought did cross my mind."

Then the painkillers finally hit and I passed out.

SUNDAY, DECEMBER 25

God rest ye merry, gentlemen, let nothing you dismay,
Remember Christ our Savior was born on Christmas Day;
To save us all from Satan's power when we were gone astray.

O tidings of comfort and joy, comfort and joy;
O tidings of comfort and joy.

—"God Rest Ye Merry Gentlemen,"
traditional English carol

CHAPTER FORTY-THREE

Christmas Day began with sparkling lights and cheerful little elves. The lights were on all the monitors attached to me, and the elves were candy stripers coming in on their holiday to cheer up the poor bedridden sufferers. With my luck, my next holiday visitor would be Rudolph the Red-Nosed Proctologist. I knew it wasn't going to be Professor Heart-Attack Higgins, though. Every time a man over forty came into my room, a Hispanic cleaning man was right behind him. Sally told me that Max had bribed the usual cleaner to take an unofficial holiday.

Angels in white changed my head and shoulder bandages, which was no joy to the world. They downgraded my medication from morphine to Percocet, which didn't make any difference, everything hurt. Getting shot sucked. This Christmas sucked! I was ready to give the Grinch a run for his money.

My cell phone went off. Max said, "I don't trust cell phones so just listen. Good call, guy. The happy couple left early this morning, to do the church thing with their maid. There was a very faint smell to the gun in question—a pump-action twenty-gauge Browning. When I felt around in the barrel, the inside of the barrel was covered with oil and gunpowder. That means it was fired after it had been cleaned. It was loaded with Remington GL20s with #7.5 weight shot. The other rifles had been cleaned, but not fired. Hope that helps. Beep."

More evidence was piling up, but I didn't know what the hell to do about it. I couldn't see One-Armed Lorraine as pump-totin' killer. And I couldn't imagine Dalton committing multiple murders to cover up for being gay. At least not in California. That's taking the fear of homophobia way too far. But I could imagine anything from the Hightower-Higgins Gang.

I don't know if it was just the adrenaline rush of getting shot, or all the medication or what, but I started to feel a gently manic rush coming on. My mind began to get clearer and clearer. At the same time I started to smile as a mild euphoria began to well up. I knew this state. Actually I lived for this state. My IQ doubled. The neurotransmitter afterburner kicked in. I could solve this thing.

I hung each fact and experience out in space. Then I began to trace the connecting lines. Some were strong. The irrelevant ones I erased as I started to see the whole picture. I kept returning to the memory of getting shot and that strange out-of-body experience that followed it. I replayed it carefully as I stared absentmindedly at the pulse monitor in front of me. The blinking red LED momentarily fascinated me. Then I saw it, and all the connecting lines blazed in light. I knew who did it. And I suspected why. Now I had to save my daughter.

Reverend Dalton's voice on the voice mail at the Church of Salvation in Christ was very helpful. "A blessing on you on this most holy of weekends. May you know Christ's love in every aspect of your life. Our Christmas Eve service begins at five on Saturday and will include our annual Christmas Devotional Offering and Banquet. Bring your appetites—our volunteers have been cooking all month for this. Sunday services begin at nine o'clock with Sunday school starting at eight forty-five. We will also have services Sunday at eleven and at one. I look forward to seeing you often this weekend. Carry the Christ child in your heart always, as you honor his birth on these special days of the year. Merry Christmas."

I called Max's voice mail. "I need backup at three o'clock this afternoon outside the Church of Salvation in Christ in Santa Cruz." Then I told him what to expect.

My next call was to Levar. "Lawrence, I need your help."

"Yeah?"

"I need you to cover my ass." I filled him in. He seemed quite amused.

Now I had to get out of here. I tried the easy way. I rang a nurse and asked her if she could disconnect me from all this drip stuff so that I could go upstairs and wish my daughter merry Christmas. No dice. She said, "I'm sorry, but the doctor's orders say complete bed rest. You can call her though."

Instead I called Sally. She'd driven home early this morning and wasn't delighted to get my call. I told her what I needed from my apartment and from my storage compartment: clothes, bandages, ten grand, a backpack, and a gun.

"No way. You've just been shot and hauled out of a wreck. You're not going anywhere!"

Then I told her why.

"You shouldn't be using your cell phone to tell me this. I'll be down in two hours."

I loved that gal!

CHAPTER FORTY-FOUR

B y one o'clock I was ready to go. It helped that Sally had been a medic in the army before her spine was crushed. She removed all the needles, patched all the holes, and redid the bandages on my head tight enough to fit an oversized red Santa's hat over most of them. Nice touch with the cap; that girl could improvise. She helped me get out of that stupid hospital gown, carefully easing a green sweater over my shoulder dressing. "I still think you're crazy, Warren. I just want you to know that. Are you sure this couldn't wait a couple of days?"

"Yep, I am. Now check the hall to make sure all's clear."

I left a little note discharging myself against medical advice, just so they didn't think someone kidnapped me. Sally came back with an "All clear." The nurses were on shift change, so the halls were empty, except for Max's maintenance man, mopping the floors. He gave us the high sign and went back to work. I looked like I was wheeling Sally to the elevators, but it was really more like I used her chair as a walker. I still was pretty woozy, not that it mattered.

The cop guarding Fran recognized me and went back to reading his *American Sportsman* magazine. Fran smiled when she saw me, until she saw both my black eyes.

"What the hell happened to you?"

"Fran, I'd like you to meet Sally McLaughlin. She's my . . . well . . . um, 'girlfriend' sounds a little juvenile and 'main squeeze' sounds too biker bitch, but you get the idea."

Sally shook Fran's hand. They just looked at each other for a moment. They both seemed to like what they saw. Then Fran looked back at me. "You look like you tried my motor-scooter-over-the-cliff trick."

"Well, the bad news is that I got shot, drove my car into a tree, and spent the night on morphine. The good news is that maybe someone will start believing me when I say that you didn't kill Orrin. Oh, and hey, merry Christmas. How did it go with the shrink?"

"Clean bill of health, thanks to Rose. There goes my insanity defense. But it means they can't take Justin away from me because I'm crazy. Rose's coaching was great. I played it just right."

"Good, but remember the price. You see her every week when all this blows over." I was being the stern dad.

"Sure, she's a prize. Are you OK?"

"I've had gentler Christmases. I'm going to try to get you out of here tonight. But I need to ask you a couple of questions just to make sure I'm right about all this."

I asked and she gave me the answers I needed.

Two more calls.

"Dalton residence." It was their maid.

"This is very important, Rita. I know Mr. and Mrs. Dalton are at church right now. I need you to contact them. Tell both of them to be at the church at three o'clock this afternoon, if they want to find out who killed Orrin Wilkins. Tell them that I need them there alone. This is Fran's father. Will you repeat that back to me?"

She did, perfectly.

"Thanks so much. Merry Christmas."

I had no idea if that would work.

Fran gave me Teddy Vespie's home number. "Vespie here."

"Hi. Ritter here, the guy you pulled out of the burning wreck."

"Hey, it wasn't burning until we got far away from it. How are you doing?" He sounded uncomfortable, which made sense since he'd both saved me and abused me in the same week.

"I just wanted to thank you for saving my life. And I want to do you a favor."

"I don't need a favor from you. I was just doing my job."

"Well, I'm going to give it to you anyway. You get to collar the person who killed your partner. And believe me she's not the woman at Coast Memorial Hospital. If you want to really fuck it up, just bring a bunch of cops with you to your church at three this afternoon, and nothing will happen. But if you come by yourself, we'll catch us a murderer."

"No deal. You're supposed to be in the hospital. Where the hell are you?"

"See you at three."

I clicked off. As Anouilh once wrote, "The spring is wound up tight. It will uncoil of itself."

CHAPTER FORTY-FIVE

I t started unwinding pretty quickly. As I left Fran's room we heard the guard's cell phone go off. As the doors to the elevator were closing we heard him call out, "Hey, you two, stop!"

We made our plans as we went down. We beat Officer Porky to the first floor and I took off to the left while Sally headed for the main door. I paused at the corridor marked RADIOLOGY, PHARMACY, EMERGENCY AND TRAUMA SERVICES. I kept in sight of the stairs. The door burst open and Mr. American Sportsman ran out into the lobby. I waited until he looked over to me and spotted me. I waved and then I started to run down the corridor. I could see that Sally was already outside, heading for her van.

I keep in good shape. I run, free climb, and do Aikido and yoga. My adversary looked like he barely waddled through his last physical. On the other hand, while he knocked back a couple of pints of beer last night, I'd spilled a couple of pints of my blood all over my car. It was a long damn corridor. So he was gaining on me.

He was right on my heels when I charged into the crowded

ER. Lots of little boys and girls had got stuck, bit, slashed, or electrocuted by their Christmas goodies this year. At least that meant he wasn't going to try to take a shot at me. Getting shot once in a twenty-four-hour period was enough. I flew out the big double doors and right into the open door of Sally's van. She stepped on it and left Tubs in the rain watching us from the sidewalk.

"He's going to call us in, Sally. There can't be that many gray vans with handicapped license plates in Santa Cruz."

"Yes, let's do something about that."

She swerved into a small residential street. Everyone was inside playing with their new toys, watching TV, pigging out, or just being thankful they didn't have to go out in this downpour. She checked her mirrors and then flicked a switch on her dashboard.

"Good-bye little wheelchair plate, hello personalized whale tail plate."

"What's it say?"

"CHANGE."

"You're scary sometimes."

"Just remind me not to park at the blue curbs."

We sat outside the church for ten minutes, waiting. Vespie's squad car was parked in front. No one else seemed interested in us or in the church. I noticed a blue Celica turn down a side street. Of course I didn't see Max. I just knew he was there. Once more I ran down all the possible options and mess-ups that I could think of. Then Sally headed for the back door of the church. I put on my backpack, tipped up the barrel of my Tom Cat to make sure a round was chambered, and stuck it, cocked and ready, in my pocket. Showtime!

CHAPTER FORTY-SIX

I walked in alone. The three of them—Dalton, Lorraine, and Vespie—had pulled chairs together and were sitting in front of the sanctuary. It was just the four of us, as far as I could tell. White lights twinkled from the decorations along the walls and the huge cross seemed to glow with a golden light. Good theater.

I slowly walked down the aisle toward my suspects. I could play this for drama, too. Vespie stood up and called out, "OK, Ritter, what the blazes is this all about?" He was much more careful of his language in church. I said nothing until I was in their midst.

I turned to Vespie. "You shouldn't have used the good reverend's shotgun to fire on me."

Lorraine cried out, "Teddy!"

He looked over at her, which gave me the time I needed to draw my gun.

"Don't reach for it, Teddy. That would be a very bad mistake to make on this most holy of days."

Dalton, to his credit, said, "Put away that gun! You're in the house of the Lord."

"Don't worry, Reverend. God won't mind me covering my butt right now. And you need to keep that gun cabinet of yours locked. Anyone can drop by while you're at your Christmas Devotional Offering and Banquet, grab one of your guns, do a freeway shooter trip, and then put it back and frame you for murder."

Vespie said, "You're crazy, Ritter. I saved your life, for Christ's sake."

Dalton scowled at him. Lorraine was even whiter than usual.

"Yes, you did. And I think it went something like this: You only wanted to scare me with that shot. You were aiming in front of my car, but I hit the accelerator instead of the brakes and drove right into it. You watched as my car went off the road. You took off toward San Jose. Then you started to feel guilty. Even after all this, you're still a cop. You couldn't just leave me there to die. So you ditched the van at the next exit, where you'd parked your squad car. You drove back to the scene of the shooting. You never expected that I would notice that yours was the only cop car that came south from Los Gatos, rather than north from Santa Cruz."

Vespie started moving to the side. "You're very bright. But I don't think you're all that tough. I don't think you have the guts to shoot an unarmed man."

He was walking away from me, up the stairs to the sanctuary. As he ascended I knew he was right. This year I'd killed two men who were trying to kill me, and those deaths still haunted me. There was no way I was going to blow away the man who had just saved my life.

He said, "I'm leaving now. You can keep all your little theories, Ritter, because they don't mean a damn thing to me."

He headed out the rear entrance. Dalton was paralyzed. Both Lorraine and I broke after Vespie. I just beat Lorraine up the stairs. She called out, "Teddy!" to his retreating back.

He was out of sight when I heard another voice call out, "Stop!" Then the sound of a gunshot filled the church.

CHAPTER FORTY-SEVEN

As Lorraine and I ran toward the back of the sanctuary we heard, "That one was for Fred Hampton and Mark Clark. This one is for Mumia Abu-Jamal."

"No more!" I yelled.

Lorraine and I burst into the vestry. A black man in a ski cap (who sounded suspiciously like a pool hustler I knew) was standing over Vespie, pointing his revolver at Vespie's genitals.

He looked up at me and said, "Ah, I was just kidding. I always wanted to say that."

Lorraine ran over to hold Vespie's head. She began crying. Slowly, a circle of red with a dark hole in the center was expanding across his upper pant leg.

From behind Levar I heard Sally's orders: "Get out of my way. I'm a doctor." She wheeled through the back door and over to Vespie. Then she grabbed her medical kit and hoisted herself off her chair and onto the floor beside him. As she cut away his pant leg she said, "Bullet went all the way through. No arterial bleeding. Grazed the major muscle group. No apparent broken bones."

She looked up at Levar as she was ripping open sterile dressings. "Nice shot."

"Thanks."

Vespie said, in a strained voice, "You're both going to jail for a long time for this."

I engaged the safety on my handgun. Then I said, "Vespie, shut up, for just a second, and maybe I won't bust you for trying to kill me." Then I looked at Levar. I took off my backpack and tossed it to him. *"Adiós, muchacho. Hasta la vista, señor."*

He looked confused for a moment. Then he looked inside. A slow smile spread across his face. "Damn, nice load of cabbage here. You're more generous than I expected. Thanks, man. You're a brother. You come down and visit me, Trav. We'll go out and get you a fish big enough to fill up *your* wall. And bring your little doctor with you."

"You got it."

He turned and walked out into the corridor.

Sally said, "Little doctor, my ass!" to his back. But she was smiling.

Dalton finally appeared at the doorway. I squatted down with Lorraine and Vespie and said, "Now let's see how we're all going to get out of this mess. I know why you did what you did, Vespie. I was getting too close. I was about to find out who killed Orrin. You told me early on. 'A man is supposed to protect his family.' That's what you were doing. Protecting your family: your boy, and your lover. Isn't that right, Lorraine?"

Vespie said, "Lorraine, don't say a damn thing!"

"Relax, Ted. None of this is admissible anyway. Let me tell you what I know. You and Lorraine had to live your relationship in secret. That's why you two would disappear on vacation together. In fact, you just came back from Hawaii, from where she brought back a violet snail shell and you brought back that tan and some particularly offensive swear words from the locals. Meanwhile Dalton was probably up in the Castro district of San Francisco, having a ball. Looking at your complexion, Reverend, you haven't seen a tropical island in your life."

Sally said, "Wound's cleaned, bleeding's stopped, but we need to call an ambulance soon."

"Just give me a couple more minutes, hon." I turned to Lorraine. "I know you and Vespie talked very recently. How else could you know that I read tarot cards for a living? Fran never told you, she was too ashamed of her good old dad. So now comes the creepy part. I don't know what he did, but somehow Orrin found out about all this, and did something unspeakable to you. What was it?"

She began to weep. "He always knew. He helped us organize our getaways, and made up lies about going on hunting trips with Larry and Teddy so that we could go do what we needed to do without anyone else knowing. I thought he was our best friend.

"He was so evil. Two weeks ago, the day Teddy and I got back from the islands, he sat in my living room and threatened me. I'll never forget it.

"He came to talk with me about Fran, or so I thought. He told me how erratic she had become. Then he said something like, 'She bruises Justin regularly. I think she needs institutionalization. Do you have a good referral of a psychiatrist who might help me get her committed?'

"I was shocked. Something felt very wrong about this. I told him, 'I understand that it's difficult between the two of you right now, Orrin. But I don't think it's quite as bad as you paint it. I know Fran, and it's true that she's troubled. But she loves her boy, and she is trying to make your marriage work. Perhaps it makes more sense for the two of you to see a counselor. I know an excellent Christian marriage counselor right here in town.'

"Then he went ballistic. He started shouting at me. 'I'm not the problem here, Lorraine,' he said, 'I'm trying to find a solution, before she permanently psychologically damages my son, or worse, crashes our car while she's drunk and kills him.'

"I wasn't having it. I told him that in every marriage both partners are responsible for the problems. I said, 'Sure, Fran is not an easy woman to live with, but she is your wife, and you can't just ship her off to a hospital to get rid of her. That's not like you, Orrin.'

"Orrin stood up and looked down on me. Then he started to hurt me. He said, 'Oh, now I'm getting the marriage lecture. You're in no shape to lecture me. Your marriage is a joke.'

"I didn't know what had happened to him. I told him, 'I love my husband very much!'

"Then he cut deep. 'Among others.'

"I asked him how he could say that. He'd been the friend of the three of us."

Then she stopped. She looked around at all of us, deciding what to say next. She took a deep breath and said, "Now I have to tell you this part, so you'll understand. If any of you speak about this outside this room I'll be ruined. But you must understand why I did what I did. This is exactly what he said to me. 'You're the righteous one, aren't you, Mrs. Incorruptible? Look, I know your secrets, and Dalton's. Oh, yes, and I know about that little prostitution charge you ducked fifteen years ago in the city. I know a ton about you, Lorraine Foster, aka Sapphire, aka Lorraine Dalton. So don't get all high and mighty with me. I can ruin you in this community and now you know it. You will come crawling to me very soon.'

"I was so ashamed. It took me years to rebuild my life, and finally I was a respected member of my community. I'd worked so hard to get away from that awful past, and now he was rubbing my face in it. I told him I didn't understand. He said, 'You don't need to understand. If you care about those you love, you just better give me what I want, when I want it. That's all you need to know. And don't say a word about our little chat, if you know what's good for you.'

"Then he swaggered out of the room.

"He called me last week and told me that unless I slept with him, he would expose everything, Teddy and my affair, Larry's homosexuality, and all those private things about my past.

"I was powerless. I didn't know what to do. God forgive me, but I hated him. I finally gave in. We met at a crappy motel in Watsonville. He came in uniform. He stripped in front of me, enjoying how much I hated this. Then he went to take a shower. He told me to get hot for him. I took his gun out of his holster and shot him in the head as he stepped out of the bathroom. Then I called Teddy and told him everything. He helped me return Orrin's squad car to the motor pool and drop his body in the river that night." She covered her face with her hands. "Forgive me, Jesus."

I said, "I don't know about Jesus, but I think the world's a better place without Orrin walking around destroying other people's lives. But it's time to face the music, Lorraine. I'll get you the best criminal attorney on the West Coast. I know him; he's going to love this case. But this afternoon you have to go to the police and confess. Just tell them you shot Orrin and then ask to speak to your attorney. He'll be down here to bail you out this evening, after he chews me out for getting you to confess. Don't you dare say anything else to the police. Nothing! Got it?"

She nodded. I turned over to Dalton and said, "Clean and unload your damn shotgun when you get home. Throw out the whole box of shells."

Sally said, "OK, Hercule Poirot, enough already. We've got to get this guy to a hospital."

I turned to Vespie, who was definitely looking paler. I hated to help out a cop who fired on me. But I had to take care of Levar, and most important, I had to free my daughter. Vespie was the key, so he was going to get a free ride this time.

"Here's your story, Ted. We were all chatting in the church when a black man in a mask came in the back door, obviously on angel dust or something, and threatened us. You tried to stop him and got shot. Then he ran away. We won't say anything about the shotgun incident. We'll do our best to get an extenuating circumstances verdict for your girl. Does that work for you?"

His eyes were still hard, but he said, "I'll do it. I get you now, Warren. You're just protecting *your* family."

My turn to nod.

CHAPTER FORTY-EIGHT

I t took us four hours to get out of town. The police had far too many questions, for which we gave very terse answers. Attorney Clyde Berkowitz, my favorite scum-sucking, bottom-feeding scavenger, almost refused to take the case when I told him how I made Lorraine confess. But then I shared some of the more delectable details of the victim's shenanigans, and he got enrolled. He ended up deciding to go for a not-guilty plea.

Busting Fran loose was much easier. Her guard had already been recalled. She smiled at Sally and me as we approached her bed. "Well, how did it go?"

I took her hand and kissed it. "You are a free lady. Pick up your bed and walk. Or better yet, just get off the damn bed and let's go have Christmas with Justin."

Since the shrink had given her a clean bill of health there was no way they could hold her. We headed back up the coast to Tara's. Sally dropped us off. She said, "Guys, I'm beat. You two go on in, and I'll see you tomorrow."

I hid my disappointment. Whatever Norman Rockwell picture I tried to paint about this Christmas kept getting fragmented. "OK, sweetie. I'll call you tomorrow morning."

Fran thanked Sally for all her help, and she drove off.

Justin was thrilled. He *sha*-ed and *mu*-ed and made some noises none of us had heard before, including, I swear, *wa wa* while looking right at me. No one would believe me. Eventually the chaos settled. We sat around Tara's tree; Justin blissfully nursed his bottle, curled in Fran's arms. Tara had decorated her tree with carved African animal figures, which made a lot of sense, knowing her. Hanging above the tree, suspended from the ceiling, was a large crystal star that swayed slightly, catching and reflecting the colors of her tree lights. All was calm, all was bright.

Fran broke the silence. "Well, thanks for everything, Warren and Tara. You've been amazing. I guess I'll be going back to Santa Cruz tomorrow, but I really appreciate all you've done."

Tara reached over and touched her arm. "No, I don't think so. I know it's hard for you to get used to, but you have a family now. What that means is you don't have to do the whole motherhood thing by yourself. In fact, you won't have to do very much of it, if you don't feel up to it."

Fran flared. "Back off, Aunt Tara. I can handle this by myself. You don't get my kid. You two a family? What a joke! A bunch of misfits, that's what we are. Am I supposed to be happy that Justin has a suicidal mother, an aunt incapable of maintaining a relationship with anything but animals, and a fortune-telling manic-depressive granddaddy? I don't see that as a big step up!"

Just then the doorbell rang. When I turned I saw the flashing lights of a squad car. Oh, no; what now? I got up to get the door.

At that moment I preferred possible imprisonment to refereeing two spitting cats.

I opened the door and looked out. Then I called back to the living room. "You two better come out here and look at this!"

I felt them move up behind me. Then I heard a loud, excited *"Ga!"*

Heather stepped out of the group in front of us and handed Justin his giraffe. She said, "We found this at our house. I think you missed this, Justin." He hugged it tightly and repeated, *"Ga."*

A burly Hispanic man who could turn invisible at will stepped forward and handed a large poinsettia to Tara. "Hello, Tara, Fran, Justin. My name is Max Valdez. This flower my people call *flores de Noche Buena,* flowers of the holy night. We tell a story that Pepita, a little peasant girl, had nothing to bring to the Christ child but a handful of weeds. She was ashamed, but then she remembered that even the most humble gift, if given in love, will be acceptable in Jesus' eyes. She dared to bring it before him, and suddenly her weeds bloomed into these beautiful flowers. This is the night for miracles. *Feliz Navidad,* Tara, Fran."

Then a cop wheeled up a high-tech three-wheeled baby carriage. "Hi. I'm Mac. I put together this stroller for Justin. It's got quick-release, sixteen-inch wheels with sealed bearing aluminum hubs, a titanium frame, adjustable shocks, and EBC oversized mountain brakes. This puppy cruises!"

Everyone laughed.

Sally made her way around the stroller and looked up at Fran. "Hi Fran. I know this is a bit much. But Hillary Clinton was right, you know. It takes a village to raise a child. Look around. This is *your* village. Believe me, Fran, any one of us would make a mess of the job of raising Justin to manhood. I know I'd botch it up, and I bet you probably know that you can't do it alone, either. But together we might just pull it off. Please, let us be your village."

Fran looked at us. She wore her customary frown. But then she looked at the customized stroller, the poinsettias, and back at Sally. Sally grinned, and, almost as if she couldn't help herself, Fran smiled back. She looked over at me and down at Justin. And then she said, "OK, come on inside. It's freezing out here."

At which point, in front of seven witnesses Justin held his giraffe out to me and said, *"Ga, wa wa."*

SUNDAY, JANUARY 1

Should auld acquaintance be forgot
And never brought to mind?
Should auld acquaintance be forgot
And days of auld lang syne?

For auld lang syne, my dear,
For auld lang syne,
We'll drink a cup of kindness yet
For auld lang syne.

—"Auld Lang Syne,"
Robert Burns

CHAPTER FORTY-NINE

Tara and I walked past the fake waterfall and climbed the hill to Viewpoint Garden. This part of the cemetery in Kensington looked out over the bay. Small plaques were set in the ground to mark urn burial places. Most of them were in Chinese and very well cared for, even in mid-winter. Fresh flowers greeted us on this New Year's Day.

Tara went over to a large boulder and sat down. She said, "Dad wanted me to be comfortable when I came to visit him. That's why he chose this spot. Good thing, too. Several ant armies are in constant warfare over this tiny strip of land. You picnic here at your own risk."

I sat next to her and looked down. There on a brass plaque was written, WALTER GREEN 1922–1993. CHERISH EVERY MOMENT YOU'RE ALIVE.

I said, "Always giving advice, that's my dad. Although that advice's a lot better than 'Pull your weight in the boat!' or 'Be a brave little cowboy!' "

Tara laughed. "Yeah, well you're lucky you didn't get 'Keep

your legs crossed until you finish college.' I think he got a little wisdom in his licentious elderhood. You know, Warren, I believe they only allow live flowers in vases as decorations. I'm pretty sure what you just tossed down there is not on the approved list."

"Tough. Let Dad appreciate it until the maintenance crew comes around."

I'd put today's *Oakland Tribune* over the plaque. It was carefully folded to expose an article.

DUO OF DEATH: A FATHER AND DAUGHTER KILLING TEAM?

After local police intercepted several cell phone conversations, they uncovered an alleged plot to murder a senior Berkeley Labs biologist, Dr. Jason McFerron. The suspects are his fiancée Julia Hightower, aka Jane Higgins, and her father, cardiologist Dr. Allen Higgins. An anonymous tipster alerted Dr. McFerron, who immediately involved the Oakland police in the successful surveillance. Police Chief Richard Plummer has hinted that this may be only one in a string of murders committed by this pair.

Tara and I looked out over the pristine view of glittering water and distant buildings and bridges. Finally she said, "Thanks for bringing those two to justice, Richard. I thought we should leave the dead behind us. But I was wrong. In Africa, the villagers were always very careful to make sure their ancestors rested peacefully. I think our father's spirit can finally relax. The people in my village would tell me that I am in your debt for doing that."

"Yes, Tara, you do owe me a favor. And I'm ready to collect it. So here's what I want. Even Justin knows my correct name. Can you please call me Warren, or at least *Wa Wa*?"

230

Notes, Apologies, and Last Mutterings

I don't know why Warren gets in such a snit about certain towns. In past books he has been unremittingly critical, in spite of the fact that Clayton is charming, Walnut Creek is a lovely place to shop, and El Cerrito is the site of some very fancy neighborhoods. Santa Cruz is all three of these things, and progressive to boot! Yet there he goes, getting the creeps about it. Go figure. I suppose Brawley isn't all that bad, either. Anyway I apologize to all these municipalities.

There are other things in this book that actually exist. Walk Circle is a cute little circular street in Santa Cruz. Roma Café and the Mediterraneum Caffè in Berkeley, and Café La La in Gualala are great coffee houses. Black Oak Books is very real. The Cheesesteak Shop serves an outstanding gourmet steak sandwich. Heather's modern version of Dante's *Inferno* was written and illustrated by Sandow Birk, and is every bit as creepy as she described it. And, yes, there is a magical pedestal tree at the Lighthouse Point Park in Santa Cruz. You've got some climbing to do to find it, but the reward is worth the effort.

Some things are completely imaginary. Alfredo's Cycles, the Coastal Memorial Hospital, the West Coast Snooker and Billiards Club, and Epic Thrash are from my fantasies. I hope the Church of Salvation in Christ does not exist, so I can continue to use that name. If it does exist, please let me know, and I will cease and desist.

As always, I encourage readers to ignore Warren's medication advice. My wife reminds me that you should show moderation in following his dietary habits also: all those cheesesteaks, burgers, and caffeine. She wants him to eat more fruits and organic vegetables.

Finally, I also apologize to the many fine men and women serving in local and federal police forces. Not a lot of good cops show up in the Tarot Card Mystery series. Warren instinctively despises almost anyone who carries a badge. But he's mentally ill. You'll just have to forgive him.

Skibbins, David, 1947-
The star

5/07

DATE DUE

May 22, 2007		
FEB 2 1 2019		

GAYLORD   #3523PI   Printed in USA